Untravelled Roads

Untravelled Roads

Tales of the Ghostly, Macabre and Weird

R.J. Meldrum

WolfStar Publishing

2015

First Printing: July 2015

ISBN 978-1-329-33468-7

WolfStar Publishing
Ontario, Canada

Cover image credit: Mellow

Cover image provided by: www.canstockphoto.com

In memory of my friend Toby

Two roads diverged in a wood, and I…
I took the one less travelled
Robert Frost

Contents

It was a bright, beautiful summer's day. That morning, Mequillen and his team had driven up from London to the northern part of Norfolk. There were three of them, himself, Don and Jackie. They worked for a television production company. The trio worked well together and they were good at their job, which on this particular occasion was to find the perfect location for a television series set in the 1950's. They were scouting out the old army and R.A.F. bases scattered around the county. First on their list was R.A.F. Highmoor.

Highmoor was an excellent candidate for the shoot. Built in 1938, it was a collection of brick and concrete buildings and prefabricated metal hangers arranged in seemingly chaotic order next to a tarmacked runway. Rotting window frames, broken windows and walls smeared with graffiti greeted the team. A derelict control tower, its windows shattered, sat mournfully gazing over the abandoned site. Highmoor had been used as a base for Lancaster bombers between 1939 and 1944. It had been abandoned for good in 1947.

Mequillen directed the others to take some photographs of the buildings, while he wandered further afield to take some measurements, possibly going as far as to plot out some likely camera angles. He walked to the edge of the runway, looking at the crumbling tarmac. His grandfather had fought in the Second World War and Mequillen remembered that the old man would sometimes show off the shrapnel wounds on his leg that he had acquired in North Africa. Must have been tough to have to fight, to kill. Mequillen could only imagine what it would have been like to be in your early twenties, climbing into a Lancaster bomber and flying off into the blue sky to drop bombs onto German cities. So many of them had never come home. Mequillen had done some background reading on the bases and the airmen, the attrition rate amongst bomber flight crews had been horrendous.

He shook his head slightly, focusing once more on the job in hand. Glancing around, he noticed something strange. There was a small, white dog sitting at the edge of the runway, about fifty feet away. It was staring down the runway, towards the east where the bombers would have come in to land, its tail wagging at a slow pace. It made for an odd sight. Mequillen, wondering if it was lost, decided to head towards it. As he got nearer, within ten feet or so, the dog noticed his presence and darted away, running between two of the nearby metal huts. Mequillen didn't chase it, knowing full well that a dog that didn't want to be caught would never be caught. He turned back to meet up with the others.

The team had opted to stay overnight in a local pub in a nearby village. There were a couple of other locations to check out in the general area before they headed back to London the next evening. As they ate their evening meal in the thatched pub, Mequillen found that his mind was still focused on the dog he had seen. It was a distinct possibility that the little dog was lost. Why else would it be hanging around an abandoned airbase? He decided to ask the barman. It was a pretty small village and he might know if a local dog had gone missing. Mequillen could never have anticipated the response he got. The barman just smiled and laughed.

"Not a lost dog, not as such. That'll be old Tommy that you saw. Little white dog, right?"

"Yes, that's right. A little white dog."

"He's not lost. He's been at the old base for over seventy years now, always in the same spot. Waiting for 'is master to return from the war."

Mequillen gaped at the man, his face flushing with anger.

"That's not funny you know. I was only concerned about the wee dog."

The barman laughed again and turned to serve the next customer.

"He isn't joking, you know," said a well-dressed man sitting at the bar, sipping Scotch. He leant over, extending his hand. They shook hands.

"Dr. Machen, local G.P."

"Dan Mequillen. I work for Source Productions down in London. We're up here scouting locations. Highmoor could be good as the location for a forthcoming television series. That's where I saw this mysterious dog."

Machen smiled.

"The tale is true you know. I didn't believe it myself when I first arrived in the area, but it really is true. Tommy was the dog's name. The story is that he belonged to a Lancaster pilot and Tommy always waited for him at the edge of the runway when his master was away on a mission. One day in 1942 his master didn't come back, but Tommy kept waiting. And waiting. Tommy died in 1946, just before the base closed for good, but his ghost remains there, waiting for the sound of the engines; the sound that signals his master is returning. But his master didn't return that one night in 1942, nor will he ever return. I guess Tommy will be there forever."

"Surely you don't believe this? You, a doctor?"

"I do, Mr. Mequillen. I really do."

Machen seemed serious and sincere,

but Mequillen simply didn't believe him. He suspected that the two locals were teasing him and dismissed their fanciful tales. But there was still the issue of the lost dog. It looked as if he would have to do something about it himself, since no-one in the village seemed willing to help.

The next morning Mequillen sent his colleagues along to the next location without him, while he returned to the airbase. He wanted to see if the dog was still there and to see if, this time, he could get a hold of it. He wanted to find out if it had tags or a microchip, so that it could be returned to its rightful owners.

Parking at the airbase, he exited the car and headed back to where he had stood the day before. Looking down the edge of the runway, he saw that the dog was sitting in the same spot. And, as before, the dog was gazing down the runway, almost as if he was waiting for a plane to return. Shaking his head in disgust at himself for being so suggestible, Mequillen walked towards the dog, but once more it noticed his presence and took off running between the buildings and out of sight. This time Mequillen chased him. Rounding the corner of one of the buildings, Mequillen experienced one of the most amazing sights of his entire life. He saw that the little white dog was running between two metal buildings, about twenty feet ahead of him. The dog headed towards a brick wall that blocked his escape route. But, as the dog approached the wall he didn't slow down or try to avoid it. Instead he went straight through, as if the solid, red brick barrier simply wasn't there. Mequillen gasped in amazement and stopped dead. It was suddenly true. This wasn't a lost dog. This was a ghost. An urge came to him. He needed to find out more about this dog from seventy years ago. He went to see Dr. Machen.

Machen wasn't surprised to see Mequillen, in fact he was rather pleased. Mequillen looked embarrassed, but described what he had seen. Machen smiled.

"You've experienced what many of us have. Tommy always follows that same route. Between the two metal buildings and then through the solid brick wall. That's why he can't be caught."

Mequillen then asked the question he felt he needed to ask. In response, Machen told Mequillen that there was only one village resident who could possibly help him. Cockerlyne. Machen told Mequillen that Cockerlyne was ninety-two years old and had been stationed at Highmoor during the war. After the armistice he had married a local girl and settled in the area. He still lived in the village, looked after by a small army of nurses and care-givers. Mequillen thanked the doctor and went on his way. He called on Cockerlyne that afternoon. He found the old man sitting on his front porch. Introducing himself, he asked his question.

"Mr. Cockerlyne, I'm interested in finding out about Tommy, the little dog who sits on the runway at Highmoor. Can you tell me more please?"

Cockerlyne grunted.

"Heard the tales, have you lad? You've seen him too, I'll wager. You're not the first to come and ask me. Many people have tried to catch him, but how can you catch a ghost? Especially one that runs as fast as he does through solid walls!"

The old man laughed at his own joke.

"The dog you saw *is* the ghost of little Tommy. I remember Tommy, remember him well from the war. I wasn't flight crew, I was ground crew loading the bombs and I remember the little fellow sitting at the edge of the runaway every time they went on a mission. I remember, clear as day, the time they didn't come back. Hamburg it was. A night raid. Out of twenty bombers, only five made it back. The flak got some of them, the fighters got the rest. Some went down over the city, others over the sea on the way home. His master was one of them that got lost. After that, Tommy just sat there day after day; we tried to get him to move, rehome him even, but he wouldn't shift. Died in that very spot in '46. We buried him right there too. The Group Captain said not to, but who cared about him, the war was over and I was being discharged the next month."

For Mequillen, there was suddenly

another question he needed to ask. An important question. Some instinct told him that it might be the most important question.

"Mr. Cockerlyne, what was the name of Tommy's owner? The pilot of that Lancaster."

Cockerlyne closed his eyes and laid back in his chair. For a few moments, Mequillen thought he'd gone to sleep, but then he spoke.

"Flight-Lieutenant Peter Winston. A nice lad, only young. Not one of the pompous, arrogant ones. He was ordinary, working class, not like those posh blokes. A good pilot by all accounts too. But when there's flak and fighters, even the best pilots can die. Not much that skill can do when you're flying straight on the bomb run. His plane was called Lucky Lucy after his girl back home. Lucky Lucy went down over Hamburg, shredded by flak. A night raid, taking off at dusk and returning at dawn. Those Germans had some very accurate flak. Just lads themselves too, defending their city. The boys who saw the Lucky Lucy go down said they saw no parachutes; likely the lads were already dead, or at least too injured to jump."

The old man shook his head.

"Horrible way to go. Horrible."

Mequillen spoke.

"Thank you Mr. Cockerlyne, thank you very much."

Mequillen had a feeling that he knew what he had to do. He would have to wait until the next day. The next morning, he made sure that he was at Highmoor just before dawn, the same time that the bombers would have returned from their night raids during the war. He saw that Tommy was still waiting in his appointed spot, still gazing hopefully into the eastern sky. There was finally no doubt in his mind that the story was true. Day after day, night after night Tommy waited for his master to return, not even death could stop him. Mequillen hoped that his plan would work and that Tommy would find peace. He walked towards the dog, speaking softly.

"Tommy, Tommy, Tommy," he sang the name of the dog. "You've been waiting so long for him, haven't you? Waiting for Peter to come home."

This time the dog did not move. Instead his ears pricked up at the sound of his master's name.

"You know what, Tommy. I think I know why you've had to wait for so long. You've needed something that no-one realised. Something you can't do yourself. They are lost out there somewhere and they need someone to call them home. To bring the Lucky Lucy back."

Tommy didn't move. Mequillen turned to the runway, looking eastwards into the sun that was peeking over the horizon. He closed his eyes and spoke.

"Lucky Lucy, Lucky Lucy, Lucky Lucy. Come home, you've been away too long. Peter Winston, Peter Winston, Peter Winston, come home. Tommy is waiting for you."

He stopped speaking and waited. There was a sound in the distance. An engine. He couldn't see properly, the light from the rising sun was making him squint and there was a haze on the runway, but he was sure it was the noise of a propeller driven plane. Unable to see it, all he could do was listen. The noise of the engines got louder and louder, and then there was a sudden squeal of tires on tarmac as the unseen plane landed. Mequillen heard the plane taxi briefly then come to a halt. The engines were shut down. He looked down at Tommy. He was still there, sitting on the edge of the tarmac, his tail wagging furiously. Mequillen knew that he would have been trained to stay put; runways were dangerous places. Voices sounded from the tarmac, but Mequillen couldn't see anything in the hazy early morning sunshine.

"Good flight, lads. That'll show those Krauts. Same again tomorrow!"

There was laughter.

"Now, where's the little fellow? Where's my Tommy?"

Mequillen looked down at the dog and Tommy finally met his gaze. His tail flicked in anticipation.

"Go to him," said Mequillen.

Tommy went.

Mequillen watched as the small white dog raced ecstatically across the tarmac towards the unseen figures. The last thing Mequillen saw was the enthusiastically wagging tail as Tommy disappeared into the sunny haze of the dawn. Mequillen heard delighted squeals and barks from Tommy and more laughter from the crew, but the noises were fading now. Soon, they faded away completely and Mequillen found himself alone on the edge of the runway of a disused airbase in Norfolk, with the sun slowly rising in the East.

Thompson took the same route into work every day and every day he got stuck in the early morning traffic. Sitting in the queue of vehicles he gazed out of his windscreen in an absent-minded and disinterested way. It was the same view every morning.

He noticed a taxi in front of him turn off the main road and drive confidently down a small lane running between two derelict warehouses. These warehouses were part of an old industrial estate that lay in an untidy sprawl on a stretch of land between the town centre and the river. Thompson had never noticed the small lane before and if it hadn't been for the taxi he would have guessed that it was just an access route to one of the long-disused loading bays. Knowing how good taxi drivers were at finding shortcuts, he made a quick decision and followed. Hopefully, it would be worth the risk. He hoped he was about to discover a new, interesting and shorter route into work. Nobody followed him.

The sudden contrast as he turned off the main highway was surprising. The lane was dark, the morning sun blotted out by the towering brick walls. There were no pavements and his side mirrors almost brushed the brick walls as he accelerated down the lane. Windows, full of shattered glass, gazed blankly at him. Moss grew on the walls, which were running with moisture. The sound of his wheels on the cobbles echoed down the street, chasing him.

The lane suddenly ended at a T-junction, presenting him with a choice, left or right. Both directions looked exactly the same. More warehouses. Unable to see where the taxi had gone he chose left, towards the town centre. This street was still cobbled but was wider than the lane, with a pavement on one side. The buildings were not so oppressive, although there was still what his wife would have called an atmosphere about the place.

He barely looked at the view as he sped down the deserted street, hoping that he had chosen the correct route. More warehouses flashed past him, remnants of an age when hundreds of men had worked in the area, unloading the ships and barges that had sailed up the river from distant lands. Exotic spices and fabrics as well as more mundane materials like tobacco, flour and grain had been stored in these huge buildings at one time. Nowadays the area was almost deserted. It had been proposed to clear the area and build smart new riverfront apartment complexes, but the economy in the town hadn't been strong enough to attract investors. Instead, the warehouses had remained. A few businesses had set up shop in the empty buildings, but the recent recession had bitten deeply and now all that could be seen were the inevitable *For Let* and *For Sale* placards posted over the faded and decaying signs that announced everything from garages to timber merchants.

Even in his anxious, mildly panicked state something caught Thompson's eye. An old man, placing a sign out on the pavement in front of a shop that lay in the middle of a row of four or five, obviously originally intended to serve the warehouse workers.

The sign read *Haircuts available all day*. The man was the first person that Thompson had seen since he left the main road. As he drove past he saw that the shop was an old-fashioned barbers. A striped wooden pole stuck out from the wall beside the door of the open shop, its paint faded and peeling. Brown, ripped net curtains disguised the inside of the shop. A sign above the door read *S. Todd and Son. Est. 1844* in antique script. None of the other shops were occupied. The old man glanced up as the car drove past, but then looked down again when it didn't slow.

Despite his rush Thompson couldn't help laughing. Talk about inappropriate! S. Todd. Like Sweeney Todd, the infamous demon barber of Fleet Street. He remembered the tale of murder and cannibalism from his childhood. He had discovered it in a museum of toys and clockwork devices. A display of novelty machines had attracted his attention. The one that featured Sweeney Todd was the Victorian equivalent of a modern arcade game. Put in an old penny and the machine would re-enact a clockwork scene. He remembered that he had enthusiastically pulled the lever on the front. Lights had sprung on, revealing a cross-section of a house, top to bottom, behind a glass front. At the top was a barber's shop, well lit and perfectly normal. In one of the chairs sat a little wooden customer, with a fat, jovial, wooden figure standing giving him a shave. The little clockwork hands of the model barber moved as they imitated the motion of shaving.

But it wasn't as innocent as it seemed. Suddenly the little clockwork razor blade was swept across the customer's throat, rather than his cheek. The little fat barber, with the same cheesy grin as before, reached down and pulled a lever on the chair. The chair and customer tipped back into the floor, to be instantly replaced with a fresh chair. There was a wait of a few seconds whilst the hidden victim underwent his fate, obviously too gruesome for the genteel Victorians. Finally, at the bottom of the house, at the kitchen level, there was an oven. Its door opened slowly to reveal a massive, gruesome pie, lit with horrible, almost fluid, red light. Obviously the victim, or at least part of him, ready to be sold in Ye Olde Pie Shop next door. At the time the clockwork toy had amused and pleasantly disgusted the child that he had been, but he remembered with a shudder the nightmares that had visited him afterwards, in which he would be the barber, slashing at the throat of his customers. The nightmares had plagued him for years, decreasing in frequency as he grew older. But they had never entirely left him.

He shook his head to rid himself of the memory. Concentrating once more on his driving, he realised that he could now see a wide bright space at the end of the street between two engulfing warehouses. As he reached the end he stopped to re-orientate himself. He laughed. Excellent! He hadn't caught up with the taxi, not even had a glimpse of it, but it had worked out all right. His car was sitting approximately two hundred yards from his work. He had managed to work his way round the outskirts of the town centre and end up close to his office, missing all the traffic in between.

For the next few weeks Thompson used his new route. Every day he would pull into the lane between the warehouses, away from the main bulk of the traffic. No-one ever followed him. He was glad, he didn't want everybody else using the route. He didn't even brag to his friends about it. In fact he never mentioned it to anybody, not even his wife. There wasn't a specific reason; he just didn't want to tell anyone.

He tried to find the name of the streets that he travelled, just for interest, but no map listed them. They were always left blank, just shown as a maze of tightly clustered lanes and streets with the massive blocks of warehouses in-between. The streets themselves had no signs. Only the warehouses themselves were marked with massive Roman numerals. Presumably that was enough for the long dead workers to find their way around.

Every day, as Thompson drove down between the towering buildings, he saw the little row of shops with the barber, who he had nicknamed Sweeney, placing his sign on the pavement. He never saw a customer, just the barber as he carried out the same sign day after day. Traditional barbers like him were a dying breed. Hidden on little back streets, their businesses dwarfed by the new salon chains. Like so many other things, they had all but passed from reality into memory. Thompson had stopped going to places like that when he had been about fourteen or fifteen. When they could no longer do the style he wanted. Instead, he had gone to the local unisex hairdressers with his mates to get a 'proper' cut, something that would get the girls. He hadn't got any, but it had been the end of his visits to the barbers. He thought that it might be nice to go back to a proper barber, to get a haircut or maybe even a shave. His mind suddenly coughed up an involuntary image of the clockwork machine, with the tiny clockwork corpse falling backwards into the floor. Well, maybe not a shave, he decided with a wry smile.

As usual the street was empty when he pulled up in front of the shop. He knew that he would be late for work, but he didn't care. He wasn't busy that morning and the boss wasn't around. There was no sign of the old man, but the sign was there, just as it always was. The morning sun didn't reach between the warehouses and Thompson gave an involuntary shiver as he slammed the car door shut and locked it. For some reason he was nervous. Butterflies danced in his stomach and he suddenly needed to go to the toilet. He stood outside the door debating for a moment, then entered.

The shop was clean and smelt fresh. It was brightly lit and every surface gleamed. Rows of bright, coloured bottles nestled in front of the highly polished mirrors. The leather chairs gleamed with polish. Thompson was impressed. The shabby exterior of the shop had given him a false impression. He had expected a dive. At the back of the shop was a doorway, covered with a bead curtain. It was through this that the proprietor, Mr. Todd presumably, made his entrance. He was neither fat nor thin, just somewhere in-between. His hair lay in thick layers on his head, looking healthy and well groomed. His skin was hardly wrinkled, it bore a healthy sheen and had few signs of ageing. Mr. Todd was old, there was no doubt, but he was also remarkably well preserved. He spoke. His voice was low and sweet.

"Can I help you, sir? Would you like a haircut or perhaps a shave?"

"Just a trim please."

"As you wish, sir. Please take a seat."

The chairs were just as Thompson remembered them from his childhood. Huge and comfortable, made from shiny burgundy leather and chrome with a bar at the bottom for height adjustment. He sat down. A clean white sheet was draped over his chest and shoulders. Mr. Todd's eyes twinkled in the mirror.

"How would sir like it?"

"Just a little off all over."

"Very well."

Thompson watched in the mirror as Mr. Todd sharpened his scissors and then picked up a comb from the counter. He began to cut. Thompson found it relaxing, just sitting listening to the quiet snip of the scissors as small pieces of hair dropped onto the sheet. He watched the barber in the mirror for a while and then began to drift off. His memory took him back to the days when his dad took him every month to the local barbers and lifted him up onto the chair. He had to sit on a cushion to get his haircut and it had been a grand day for him when he was big enough to sit on the chair without needing the 'baby' cushion.

Thompson woke with a start. He glanced at Mr. Todd, ready to make a joke about falling asleep, but the joke froze on his lips. He looked round the shop in panic. It had all suddenly changed. The clean fresh smell was still there, but wasn't there something else underneath that? Something that smelt faintly rotten and disgusting. And didn't those bottles seem to be filled with oily, slimy fluids and laboratory specimens, rather than just normal hair tonics. Even the smile on Mr. Todd's placid face alarmed him. It was the same smile as before, but wasn't it just a little bit too broad and a bit too friendly? As if the man had something to hide. Thompson spoke quickly and without thinking, saying the first thing in his mind, just to hide his alarm.

"You have a strange name for a barber, don't you Mr. Todd?"

"Do you think so, sir? Why's that?"

"Well, S. Todd. You know, Sweeney Todd. The murderer."

"Oh yes, sir. That's been said many times to me, over the years. Most of my gentlemen make a joke about it."

"But isn't it bad for business? Having a name like Todd. After all he was a notorious murderer."

"Oh yes. I see what you mean. It's interesting that you should mention that. You know sir, the original Sweeney wasn't really a proper murderer. Just a businessman who spotted a good way to make money. His main failing was that he got greedy. Started to kill too many people. That's when he got caught. It would have been better if he had stuck to his original plan."

"You seem to know a lot about him. You weren't related to him were you?"

Thompson said it jokingly, but the response was serious.

"Of course I am, sir." The barber seemed almost surprised that Thompson didn't realise. He continued speaking.

"It's a funny tale. You see sir, back when old Sweeney was about to be executed he made a pact with his only son. A son, who still loved his Da, even after all the rest of his family had deserted him. They made a pact to carry on the business. To keep the tradition alive. The tradition of the barber shop. But his son was also to keep the other tradition alive. Not to sell it, no, that's what got his Da caught. Just to take it once in a while and to keep it all for himself. After all, his son had been brought up on his Da's special pies and once you get a taste for that particular meat it's impossible to enjoy anything else. The son had to move, of course, so he left London and came up north to set up this very shop. Finding a wife wasn't difficult and once a son had been born, well, she was no longer needed. That son, born of Sweeney's son, was brought up to take over the business when his Da died. On his deathbed his father passed on to him the secret of the pies that the child had been fed on since he was a nipper, and a pact was made again between father and son to carry on with the tradition. It's been the same ever since. But, alas, now it's nearly over. I'm the last of the line. My poor wife was barren and there was no divorce in my day, so no son for me. The business will be finished once I'm gone."

"What a load of crap! Are you trying to scare me or something? Is this how you treat all your customers? Well I'm not putting up with it. I'm off. Don't expect to get paid for this."

Thompson started to get up, grateful for an excuse to leave, but he was held down on the seat by the barber.

"I'm sorry. You can't leave yet. In fact, you can never leave. I would have thought an intelligent man like you would have realised the truth in what I was telling you. I'm sorry, but I can't resist you. It's a rare day when I get one as young as you. You look well fed, your meat will be most fragrant and succulent. I'm sorry."

The barber's hand no longer held scissors, but a cut throat razor. The blade sparkled in the light.

"Are you insane?"

"No, sir, I'm not. But that won't stop me."

Thompson struggled vainly against the strength of the barber. He could not move. Sweeney stared wildly at him, his eyes burning. Thompson was squashed further down into the chair, his face pressed against the armrest. His cheek was pulled back from his teeth as more pressure was applied. He realised sickeningly that the barber was trying to pin him down to get a clear shot at his throat. The realization gave him a huge burst of adrenaline and he pushed with all his might against the seat cushion. Sweeney, moving the razor from his left to right hand, was caught at exactly the wrong moment by the thrust. He was pushed backwards by the force of Thompson's body and thumped against the mirror, shattering it and throwing glass everywhere. The razor skidded from his hand onto the floor. Sweeney recovered himself quickly and moved forward to make a grab for it, but Thompson, his muscles still bursting with power, was already scrambling to the floor and got to it first. Without aiming the blow, he slashed upwards at the barber as Sweeney reached down towards him. The razor caught Sweeney across the face, leaving a wide, shallow slash on his cheek. Sweeney reeled backwards and, without thought, Thompson slashed at him again. This time the razor caught the barber across the throat. Blood immediately stained the front of the white tunic that the barber wore and, with blood pumping from the wound, Sweeney quickly and silently died. Slowly, incredibly slowly, the body fell against the wall, slid down and slumped onto the floor. Thompson stared at it in amazement. Then, he passed out.

He couldn't have been out for more than a few seconds. As he opened his eyes he saw Sweeney still staring blankly at him. He saw the blood and the dead flesh. He felt no regret, just amazement that someone could die as easily as Sweeney had. He shook his head incredulously, this was the man that had been going to eat him. Cook him in a pie and eat him. Had the barber been insane, or had his story actually been the truth? It seemed so unbelievable, like something out of a horror film. Generations of the same family line, stretching out over a century and a half, passing a secret knowledge from father to son. It almost seemed a shame that the line had ended. That there would be no more Sweeney Todds. But it was still incredible. Despite himself, his mind wandered. Thompson wanted to know what drove that desire to eat human flesh. He wondered what it tasted like. Was it different to other meats? Why was it so special? The immediate desire to run from the shop, to escape, was balanced by curiosity. His curiosity got too much and, leaning forward towards the corpse, he stared at the slash in the throat. Blood still oozed from the wound, although the heart had long stopped pumping. Without thinking Thompson dipped his finger in the fresh blood and tasted it. He expected to be revolted, to throw up, but instead it tasted wonderful, sweet and metallic. His stomach rumbled, but he didn't notice. Using a small piece of broken glass he cut a sliver of flesh from the wound. It was dark red and well-marbled, like a good steak. After a moment's hesitation he slipped it into his mouth, held it for a few seconds and then swallowed. The meat was fragrant and delicately flavoured. His stomach rumbled for more. This time he was aware of it. An image sprang to mind. He imagined a nice steak pie, piping hot and full of delicious fragrant chunks. A special pie. It wouldn't take too long to cook. Thompson guessed that below the shop there would be a nice big oven. It may even be already lit, waiting for the next batch. With no small amount of effort, he dragged the body to the chair and flopped it over the arms, careful to make sure that none of the limbs were overhanging. Then he pulled the lever that he knew was hidden under the seat. The chair disappeared into the floor to be replaced by a fresh one. Thompson walked to the shop door and locked it. Then he turned and walked through the beaded curtain at the back of the shop.

There's a new barber at Mr. Todd's shop now. A much younger man. When asked by the few regulars to the shop he merely smiles distantly and says that he is the young Mr. Todd. He is the son mentioned on the sign outside and he has taken over the business now that old Mr. Todd has retired. He then asks in a sweet, low voice whether sir would like a haircut or…perhaps a shave.

I

Magic was gone, forgotten by time and by culture, but one last magician remained. On this planet, this desert planet where the cities stood isolated and alone like dusty sentinels, he was the last of them all.

He stood in the centre of the room. The darkness around him hid the wonders contained within that one solitary storeroom, in the basement of the building deep in the heart of the citadel, a building that had once been known as The Majestic Magic Club. He moved his arms, reaching out to hold the darkness. Capture it. Darkness was his best friend. It had once hidden his illusions and now it hid his thoughts.

He lived in the darkness now, only leaving its embrace occasionally to find food. He wasn't scared of the citadel outside, full of the scum and the poor of the city. He wasn't scared of anything, except the future. Now that there was nothing for him. Now that all his friends were gone.

He had been a magician, back in the

past. Not a great magician, not even a good one some would say. But he had been a member of the Magic Circle, and that had made him a magician. He remembered his old show in the summer time, with the pavilion filled with kids and noise. Good times. Well, not that good. He had always suspected that the audience knew the trick behind his illusions. That they could see the mirrors, catch the sleight of hand. They had never said so, always laughing and clapping at his antics, but deep down he felt their laughter was a sham.

But that had been years before, decades. Now it was different. The city was stratified, rich and poor living separate lives in separate areas. The poor occupied the centre of the city, the old downtown area, while the rich lived in the outskirts and suburbs. It was worse now than it had ever been and neither side wanted magic tricks or illusions anymore. The rich were obsessed by technology, clothes and cars. The poor were too wretched and apathetic to care about anything apart from their drugs. The magic was over and all the other magicians long dead. He was the last. The last one that still clung to the magic of glittering costumes and disappearing girls. But he was old and with him, The Great Pingini, it would all die.

He walked into the darkness, past familiar objects. Cabinets, adorned with wonderful swirling symbols and cryptic figures. Mirrors and tables, with hidden levers and switches. Glass fronted boxes for the escapologists to wriggle free from. All the paraphernalia of the illusionist. Some of the stuff was his own. The rest were the remnants of the shows that had run at the Majestic during its heyday.

He touched the surface of a human sized cabinet, stroking his hand down towards the base to feel the tiny lever that would perform the trick. He touched a collection of dusty silk scarves, their colour faded by use and time, then a collection of swords, their edges dulled by rust.

A gleam from within the mass of fake swords caught his eye. He reached in and pulled it out. This sword was different; its blade was razor sharp, the edges catching the red light of dawn from the solitary basement window. He stared at it fascinated. On the blade were symbols, hieroglyphic designs. Pictures that meant nothing to him, but that seemed so familiar. The handle was covered with soft leather, its shape fitted his hand perfectly. The golden hilt was bejewelled with bright white gems.

He put the sword up to his face, feeling the strength within the blade. He felt its coldness, its power, its warmth. Yesterday, when he had walked past the swords, it hadn't been there. This was it. This was the sign he had been waiting for. The sign to start performing once more. It was ordained. The people would come and experience the forgotten wonder of magic once more. The sword spoke to him and he listened to the plan. It was simple.

He stood in the dusty room, surrounded by his past, and tears coursed down his withered face.

II

Sheriff Paggett spoke.

"I hate these drug sweeps into the citadel, why do I always, always get chosen?"

He rose and scratched himself. His breath was stale and his clothes were full of body odour. There had been a three day push to rid the outside ring of the citadel of pushers. Some had been arrested, more killed and the rest scattered, forced to leave their happy pills behind. But it wasn't enough. There was still more to do. An informant, newly arrested, had told them about a huge load of pills just recently arrived in the citadel from the Northland. One complete consignment. Paggett knew for a fact that the guy who received the information wouldn't have to risk his neck in the citadel on the strength of a sold-out pusher's word. But it had to be done, just to make sure that none of the pills got through to the city, to the important citizens. They didn't care about the inhabitants of the citadel itself, just the population that mattered.

As a matter of routine the boss had ordered a crew to go with him. Not that those mutants were much more pleasant than the scum in the citadel.

Picking up his gun he walked out his office, checking the lock was in place. He walked to the toilet and took a cubicle. Removing his dispenser from an inner pocket he took a snort from the contents. His mind buzzed then settled down to a pleasant hum. Now he was ready to face the citadel again.

III

The Great Pingini left the basement and headed up the stairs to the main part of the club. He passed through the theatre, where the public performances had taken place. The power to the citadel had been cut off years before and the windowless room lay in almost total darkness, but he knew the layout by heart and avoided all the tables and chairs. He passed through an inner set of doors and into the reception. In front of him lay the main entrance to the club. He stared at it for at least half an hour. The sword, clutched in his left hand, was forgotten. There was no other way, he knew that, but still he hesitated. But there was no point. Eventually he would die and then the magic would be lost for ever. It was better for him to finish it this way. He pulled open the door and stepped outside for the first time in weeks. The dull morning light of the citadel welcomed him. He closed and locked the door of the club for the last time.

Filth and decay lay scattered around him. The windows of the ruined buildings stared at him as he walked past the inhabitants of the citadel lying in the streets. The dead on the pavement lay close to the living, identical in appearance and smell. All of them the scum of humanity, thrown or forced out of the city by the Sheriffs. In the distance he could just see the gleaming spires of the surrounding city, shining like burnished silver through the haze of pollution. Smoke trailed upwards somewhere to the west, probably a funeral pyre. He walked past hovels, constructed from the remnants of once proud buildings destroyed by war and time. Screaming kids sat in the dirt outside these places, while parents sat in a drugged haze within. The citadel was sick, and there was only one medicine; the happy pills. Cheap and effective, they were the only thing that could keep reality in the background. It was all they knew, from birth till death.

The citadel. Where the drop-outs and

exiles came to die.   But now there was another medicine that was going to cure the ills of the citadel.

The Great Pingini walked to an open section of ground, not far from the club. Bricks and wood lay scattered around the site. On the ground lay dozens of small metallic objects; removed from underground stores; they had been dumped when it was discovered that they held no value.   Pingini had seen them before but had never realised their significance.   Ancient artefacts of a past civilisation.   They had lain on that waste ground for years, ignored by the adults or poked at by the kids.   No-one knew what they were, but the sword somehow did.   The sword had told him what they were.   And what they could do.

He found one in better condition than most, well away from the rest, lying on a pile of bricks.   A scruffy child was sitting on it, eating something indescribable.   It was wearing almost nothing, despite the cold of the morning.   Dirt was plastered over its body and boils and sores festered on its skin.   He chased it away.   As the child moved off the metal object, he flicked a rusty blade out towards Pingini, but it was just for show. The child wasn't threatened by the old man. In fact, it was the magician who, by rights, should have been scared of the child. It was probably the sword that swayed the child's mind against attacking.

Pingini bent to look at the metallic object. It didn't look like anything in particular. It was a metal cylinder, greyish in colour. It looked like a garbage bin, but the sword told him that it was an ancient weapon. Something called a warhead. The Great Pingini had no idea what that word meant. He gazed at the object. For a moment he was tempted to disbelieve what he had been told, but he couldn't. The sword was telling him the truth. He knew that. This was the device that was the source of the magic for his trick. The object was dangerous. Dangerous and volatile. He touched it, half-expecting Death to take him there and then.

"What you doin', old man?"

The Great Pingini, who had been expecting to meet Death himself, came extremely close to soiling his trousers. He whirled around, ready to defend himself with the sword. The child, the one chased away a moment ago, stood in front of him. It had come back for a closer look.

"What you doin', old man?" the child repeated.

"Don't call me that. My name is the Great Pingini."

"What you doin...Pin?" the child said again, unsure of the long name.

"Go away. It's nothing to do with you, child."

The child didn't move.

"What do you want that for? Is it food?"

"Of course not. Go away," said the Great Pingini, determined not to be dragged into a conversation with a moronic citadel child.

"Tell us then, Pin."

"It's magic. Do you know what magic is?"

"Is it food?"

The child was too young to remember. The Great Pingini's heart was filled with sadness. But also certainty. This child would see a magic act before too long.

"No, it's not food. It's better than food. If you help me I will let you watch."

The child stared at him without moving, its tiny, wizened face full of transparent doubt. The Great Pingini turned away from it and started to lift the object into a bag that he had brought. The object was a lot heavier than it looked and he struggled. He was about to drop it when he felt the child help to support its weight with his tiny muscles. Together they managed to get it into the bag. The Great Pingini slung it carefully over his shoulder. It was heavy, but there wasn't far to go.

"Thank you child. Come along and you can help me more later on."

"Okay, old man. As long as there's food."

IV

Paggett jumped out of the C-carrier. The crew followed and assembled soundlessly on the road. They were just on the outskirts of the citadel. No man's land. The sight of the deserted buildings sent a shiver down Paggett's spine. The drugs were starting to wear off and he didn't feel comfortable. Down the street in front of him, under a black haze, lay the citadel, the rotten heart of the city. There was no clear demarcation between the city proper and the citadel, but you always knew when you were in it. Filthy, unkempt, diseased people living horrible, addicted lives in ramshackle huts amongst the ruins. The criminals and exiles of civilisation, spending their time stealing and begging from each other.

As you went further into the citadel it got worse. Paggett had never been more than two miles into it, no further than the outer ring, but that was bad enough. The citadel itself extended for about another ten miles, getting worse as you headed towards the centre. God alone knew what it was like in there.

"Don't know why they don't just bomb the place," Paggett muttered to himself.

"Pardon, sir?"

The nearest crewman had overhead.

"Nothing. Shut-up."

"Yes sir!"

The crewman saluted, his polished weapon gleaming in the sunlight. Paggett pulled his own weapon out of the holster at his side and checked the firing mechanisms and the ammunition. He clicked the safety off.

"We have to walk from here. The carrier is too easy a target for the scum in there. Stick to the side of the ruined buildings and watch my signals. Shoot anything that comes near you. Don't take any risks. I'm not spending the rest of my career filling out forms explaining why you lot got killed today. We've got three main target areas, hangouts of the suspects. If we find anybody in them, kill them. If we get ambushed, kill them. We're only after the consignment and we've got enough suspects already. "Let's go."

The fire-team moved off, falling into strict patrol formation. Paggett went second in line. The scum of the citadel always killed the front man first. He sent the smart-ass trooper ahead, the one who had asked 'pardon'.

V

The Great Pingini had the perfect location, the old market lying on the edge of the outer ring. Years before it had been the hub of this part of the city when the word citadel had actually meant something. Traders had used to come from all over the colony to ply their trades and to sell wonderful, magical things. The Great Pingini remembered coming to the market as a young man, full of life and ambition and ready to take on the world. He had been sure that he was going to be the greatest magician alive, bragging and showing-off to the girls around him. The Great Pingini smiled to himself. That had been a long time ago. Time and experience had shown him the true path of his life. Not so great, but now, at the end, at last worth something.

The streets weren't too busy as the curious pair shuffled painfully and slowly towards the market; the old decrepit man, bearing his burden and the street child, filthy and dishevelled. A few scruffy individuals shambled past them, but barely raised their heads. One or two pushers eyed them suspiciously, but since the raids of the previous days they weren't going to attract any attention to themselves. They just checked the two out briefly, then slid back into the shadows.

The Great Pingini stopped. They had been walking for about two hours without a break. He was thirsty and felt his muscles screaming for rest.

"I have to sit down for a while. And find something to drink."

He felt that he should have thought of it himself, about bringing some water, but it had never occurred to him. The sword had not suggested it, but it had no need for such things, did it? He staggered into the nearest building, with the child following behind.

"Is this where the food is, Pin?"

The Great Pingini flopped onto some rubble, his old bones complaining bitterly.

"You must fetch some water for me, boy"

The child looked at him for a moment then disappeared. The Great Pingini slumped back onto a charred piece of wood and closed his eyes, not daring to sleep. The sword lay across his lap, his burden at his side. The child returned a few moments later, bearing a rusty tin full of rusty water. The Great Pingini drank it all.

"Thank you, my boy. I must sleep for a while. Keep watch, and let no man come near. Wake me if they do."

"Okay, Pin. I will."

The Great Pingini sank into a dream-filled sleep where he performed to a packed audience, all laughing and clapping at his amazing tricks.

VI

The mission was going okay. One minor skirmish with no casualties so far. The scum ambushing them had underestimated their firepower and had paid the price for their error. Paggett smiled. Ten citadel scum dead and their heads to prove it.

The first two hideouts of the pushers had proved worthless. After the recent raids they hadn't been re-occupied. The buildings had been picked over by scavengers searching for drugs or food. Even the bodies of the men killed by the Sheriffs had been taken. The consignment hadn't been there. The team was now on their way to the third location, down by the old market. Paggett remembered it from his early childhood, full of light and noise. It was a place that he had visited with his grandfather. He pushed the thought away and concentrated on the mission ahead. The day was beginning to draw towards its end and he wanted to finish and leave before it got properly dark, but they needed to take a break. Dispensing justice was thirsty work. Paggett waved to the team to stop them.

"Take a break for a few minutes. Set sentries."

Paggett wandered off on his own,

towards a wrecked building. A trooper ran up behind him.

"Be careful, sir. You shouldn't stray too far from the main team."

"I know that. I'm just scouting the land. Go back to the rest."

The trooper turned and double-timed back to the group. Paggett found a hidden corner, well away from the team and huge a huge snort of powder. He felt magically better, his head clearing in an instant. He headed back.

"Mount up, we're off. Last hideout and then we're done. We're heading near to the old market."

The fire-team jumped at the order and reformed into the patrol grouping. They walked on towards the old market as the late afternoon sun faded. This was about as far into the citadel as the Sheriffs dared to go. Beyond the market, the citadel got seriously unpleasant.

VII

The Great Pingini woke, his back stiff and his muscles crying out. It took him a moment to re-orientate himself. For a second or two he was still back at the show surrounded by praise and laughter, but the feeling quickly dissipated. His hand still rested on the object and the sword still lay across his lap. The child, alerted by a sixth sense, looked over at him. He had done as he had been told and had kept watch.

"How long have I slept?"

"A few hours I reckon Pin. The dark is coming."

The Great Pingini felt a moment of panic. Was it too late? Had he messed up the trick? He put his hand on the sword. It was alright. The sword told him that it was perfect timing. Most of the citadel people came out at after dark. He would have a large audience for his trick.

"Come child, we must go."

"When will there be food, Pin? I'm starving."

The Great Pingini touched the child's head.

"It will be alright soon. You won't have to worry about it soon. Come on."

The pair headed out of the building. The Great Pingini shouldered his burden once more. The streets were busier as darkness approached and the pushers were more visible. The Great Pingini hid the sword in the folds of his long coat. He didn't want to be murdered for it.

When they got to the old market it was busy with people. The light was leaving the sky, the golds and reds of the sunset reflecting as multi-coloured streaks on the wet cobbled surface of the market square. The Great Pingini stooped and spoke some whispered instructions to the child who then ran off. Pingini walked to the middle of the market and stood, his arms spread wide. He spoke, using his theatrical voice; projecting it across the square as if he was young again.

"People of the citadel!"

Some people paused to look, but not many. He continued.

"Tonight there will be an amazing spectacle performed within this very place! Tonight you all have the chance to see the most incredible thing in the world! A forgotten art!"

More people were stopping to listen and a small crowd was gathering around him.

"All of you should, nay must, attend! You will see such a sight as never seen before within this city! A sight which you will not believe! I do not ask for any money from you, nor do I ask for food. I only ask that you witness this amazing spectacle!"

VIII

Paggett stood on the street, keeping an eye out. He glanced towards the sky. It was starting to darken. The streets were already filling up, although the scum would still avoid the troopers. He could hear the team ransack the building that housed the third and last hide-out. Again it looked like nothing was going to be found.

Someone screamed behind him, followed by a shot. Paggett smiled. Sounds like the boys had found someone to play with. He had grown to like them. They really weren't too bad for mutants. Well-disciplined and vicious. Just the way he liked them. He took another snort from his canister, then walked down to pick up his fire-team.

They exited the building, the team hugging the walls as they headed through the market and out of the citadel. The people moved quickly out of their way. Towards the centre of the market square Paggett saw that there was a group of people standing together. Someone was speaking to the people in a loud and powerful voice. Paggett's suspicions were raised. The last thing that the Sheriffs needed was some rabble-rouser doing their stuff in the citadel. Last time that had happened there had been full scale riots for three weeks. He motioned the team forward to investigate. As they got close Paggett saw that it was some old geezer with some sort of performance. The people around the troopers ignored their presence. It was obvious that they were enthralled by the whole thing. Paggett listened curiously.

IX

The Great Pingini stared at the crowd in front of him. Word had spread quickly and there were about two hundred people in the old market square. The child, just as he had been asked, had found an old table, the wood marked and torn. Probably an original part of the old market stalls. On it The Great Pingini had placed the precious object and had covered it with a scavenged sheet. The heart of the trick. He put the sword beside it. The child, eager to see what was going to happen, stood peering over the edge of the table. The Great Pingini could see just his eyes and a swatch of dark hair.

It was a simple trick, maybe too simple, but the sword had told him that it was impossible to fail. He was just to follow instructions. The Great Pingini knew what to do. There would be no escape for him, he had worked out that much for himself, but he didn't mind. He felt no fear, just a longing to die. Maybe to be with his friends, perhaps just to sleep. He was too old to live. Whatever had spared him from death all this time, he didn't know. Maybe it was fate, maybe something worse. Probably just luck. It didn't matter. It was over for him. He was dead already. It was the children, like the one beside him that he felt sorry for. But the sword had told him that there was to be no mercy. And there wouldn't be. Better for them all to die, rather than live in a world without magic. The Great Pingini spoke.

"Welcome to you all. Welcome to the Last Magic Show. I know that some of you, most of you perhaps, have forgotten magic. This is not your fault, the world has moved on too far. But fear not, tonight you will become briefly reacquainted. For tonight I will draw upon my unique skills to perform a feat unparalleled in history. Tonight with the aid of my special magic device and magic sword I will make the whole city disappear! Yes, my dear friends, believe it or not, before your very own eyes this beautiful and magnificent city of ours will disappear. Not even the great men of magic, names such as Houdini, could have possibly dreamed of possessing the power to make an entire city disappear, but tonight I have that power! Believe me, my good friends, when I say that this is no shoddy illusion. This is real, powerful magic."

He paused so that the crowd could digest his words.

"And so without further ado, I will perform the trick."

He nodded to the boy who removed the sheet from the table. The crowd stood still, enthralled. The Great Pingini picked up the sword, feeling it vibrate in his hands. Its voice was silent now, the trick was nearly over. He held the sword above the object. In his mind he could hear a drum roll and patiently waited for it to finish. He gazed at the audience, in an agony of suspense. Had they guessed the trick already? Would they be interested?

Paggett was. He was terrified. Unlike the troopers and people around him, he knew exactly what the object was. And what it could do. If it detonated, the old man was right. The city would disappear; in a cloud of irradiated smoke. He pulled out his pistol and fired, knowing that it was already too late.

The bullet from Paggett's gun took the Great Pingini in the throat. Blood, flesh and skin exited from the back of his neck. Only a gaping hole was left. The Great Pingini felt nothing, nothing at all. As he fell, his nerves and muscles letting go all at once, he saw the unsupported sword, brilliant despite the darkness, fall gracefully, magically towards the warhead. The blade, propelled by an unseen force, pierced the outer casing and penetrated through to the heart of the weapon. The tip of the blade was driven straight through to the table beneath. There was a brief moment of stillness, with a hushed silence settling over the audience. Then, oblivion. The Great Pingini saw the light, the fantastic light, and knew that the trick had worked. He, the worst, best and last magician in the world, had succeeded. The last magic trick, to make the city disappear, had worked. He smiled. And then, like the rest of the city, he died.

The fire-door was unlocked, as he had been told it would be. He pushed it open very carefully, suspicious that he was being set up. He didn't want to spend any more of his life in the joint. There was a brief hesitation, but then his simple, animal instincts made a balanced judgement. No-one had enough of a grudge against him to frame him and he needed the money. He really needed the money. He entered the museum.

It was 3 a.m. Outside, the dark streets were empty. The late night revellers had finally gone home and it was still too early for the street cleaning crews and early morning commuters. He took one last glance at the outside world, then the fire-door closed behind him.

As his eyes adjusted to the gloom he thought back to the previous day. He'd been contacted by his usual guy, Bob. Bob was an arranger, a conduit between those who needed scores doing and those who could do them. He thought back to their conversation.

Bob had been sitting in his filthy basement office as usual.

"Okay Paul, this is an easy one. In and out. Five hundred if you do it right."

Back in the day he would have laughed at five hundred, but these days he couldn't be so choosy. He replied.

"What's the job? I'll decide if it's easy or not."

Bob looked at him, a slimy, knowing look that said everyone knew good old Paul was in the hole to Fabio the bookie to the tune of six thousand and if he didn't pay it back soon then a couple of Fabio's goons would visit him and leave him permanently unable to walk. Good old Paul was in a tough spot and Bob knew it.

"It's a straightforward heist. From the Museum of History on Broad Street."

"That place? Full of old bones and broken pottery?"

Bob smiled. Smirked.

"I didn't know that you were so cultured."

Paul's face flushed red.

"I remember it from high school. We went there once. It was boring."

"Said the true connoisseur," replied Bob. Paul just looked at him. He was used to Bob's insulting ways, but he couldn't let himself rise to it. Bob continued.

"The client is wealthy collector of artefacts. In the museum is something that he wants. You collect it and deliver it to him."

"Museums have got good security. Tough to just to walk out with something."

"You'll go in at night. A fire-door will be conveniently left open for you, with the alarm disabled. You go in, take the items and drop them off at a pre-arranged spot. Easiest five hundred you'll make this month."

"Sounds too easy. What's the drawback?"

"No drawbacks, I just need some-one to disable the cabinet alarm, take the items and drop them off."

"Security?"

"Front desk with hourly patrols. Got the timing, so you can avoid them."

"Cameras?"

"Of course, but our inside man will ensure that they are disabled."

"Why can't this guy do the job?"

"Because these items are valuable and rare. Once they're taken all the staff will be under scrutiny. Our guy is making sure that he is very, very visible tonight. In fact, he has gone on vacation and will be able to prove that fact once the heat comes down on the museum."

Paul paused. It all sounded plausible.

"Okay, I'm in."

"Good. Now here are the details of the items."

The rest of the conversation was all business.

With the fire-door closed behind him, Paul found himself facing a dark corridor. The place smelt musty, forgotten. It was absolutely silent, no noise from the outside world disturbed this place of study and reflection. He checked his map, a scrap of hand-drawn paper illuminated by his phone. Down to the end of this corridor, turn west into the South and Central American room and then straight through that into the European exhibits.

The items were on the south side of that room, next to the stairs that lead up to the Arabic room. He set off down the wooden panelled corridor. There were high windows that allowed some of the illumination from the street lights outside to help guide him. If it hadn't been for that dim illumination, his journey would have been more or less in darkness. The wooden floorboards beneath his feet made no noise as he crept forward on rubber-soled shoes. His mind wandered.

Earlier that evening, in his dismal one room apartment, wiling away the long hours waiting for the clock to crawl around to 3 a.m., Paul had done some background reading about the items he was about to steal. The internet was very informative. The items that he was being paid to remove from the museum were called The Silences. Three tiny figures, no more than four inches high. Crudely made from pottery, they were supposed to be around three hundred years old. Paul read that the configuration of these figures was unusual. Normally the sequence for these types of figures was see no evil, speak no evil and hear no evil, with the eyes, the mouth and the ears of each figure covered in turn. For these particular figures it was different, all of them had their mouths covered. None of them were depicted as being able to speak and that's what made them so interesting, valuable and collectable. They had been nicknamed The Silences by a collector in the 1960's. The name was very apt and had stuck.

Their origin was unknown, but it was considered by experts that they had been made in Germany in the late 1700's. They had surfaced in the late nineteenth century, having been discovered during the excavation of a church crypt in Bavaria. Bequeathed to a museum in Munich, they had sat unnoticed and unstudied until 1945, when they disappeared. At that point they were just a curiosity and in the chaos of Europe at the end of the war, no-one sought to find and recover them. In 1956, a French antique dealer had found them for sale in a flea market just outside Paris. He recognised them, having seen them on display in Munich in 1936. He bought them for a song and placed them for sale in his antique shop. Since that time they had been acquired by various private collectors and public museums, moving from owner to owner, gradually increasing in value as their rarity and antiquity was acknowledged and increasingly sought after. Now they were here in the Museum of History, having just been purchased using a government grant.

Paul had been intrigued to find out that there was a dark history associated with these little figures. He had been half-amused and half-disgusted as he read the so-called genuine tales associated with The Silences. There were dozens of such tales on the internet surrounding these little figures.

Apparently, a lot of the owners of the figures had died in mysterious, violent ways or had simply vanished. Some of the conspiracy nuts on the internet reported that some people had even mysteriously disappeared after merely viewing the figures. Nonsense, Paul had thought. He had closed his laptop, shaking his head at the naivety of some people. Some folk believed anything and everything that they read on-line. But not him, he was too sensible.

Paul reached the end of the corridor and turned left, careful to make as little noise as possible. The quiet in the museum was so deep, so intense that even the tiniest squeak of a shoe would be a huge, vast intrusion into the silence. There was absolutely no sound from anywhere in the building; no wind against the window panes, no creaking of wood as the temperature changed, no skitter of mice. Nothing. The silence was so profound that he could almost hear it.

Paul was finding it unnerving. Not the most imaginative of people, even his crude senses were tingling at the complete absence of noise. He had to physically stifle the urge to make some sort of sound, to cough or to mutter to himself. He wanted to giggle.

He entered the South and Central American room, pausing on the threshold to check that the room was empty. It was a large space, full of display cases and cabinets, containing a multitude of treasures. There were bigger windows in this area, so it was easier to see where he was going. He traversed the room without paying any attention to the contents. He was entirely focused on the goal and the money that he would be paid for successful delivery. And, even if he wouldn't admit it to himself, he was trying to ignore the all-encompassing silence. It was still unnerving him. He was on edge. He tried to smile. Here he was, in the most silent of places, trying to steal three little figures called The Silences. He wasn't immune to the irony of the situation. His head was beginning to hurt.

He headed through the open doorway that marked the transition between South America and Europe. He had successfully reached his destination; all he had to do now was find The Silences, silence the display case alarm, take the items and get the hell out. He was relieved, this place was freaking him out. The silence weighed down on his mind, sweat popping out his forehead. His head was thumping with pain.

He found the display case and, without really thinking about what he was doing, bent forward to study the three little figures sitting all by themselves on a piece of black cloth. They weren't very impressive. Three little pudgy robed figures, each with his little mouth covered with both hands. Monks, maybe? He thought about the creepy tales surrounding these little guys. The deaths. The disappearances. Urban legends, had to be. He didn't believe such nonsense; his take on it was that if a group of statues managed to survive for over three hundred years then simple chance would occasionally place them in locations where bad things happened. It was all, no doubt, simple coincidence.

He found himself staring intently at the figures. His heart suddenly froze. He wasn't sure whether it was his headache or the poor lighting, but he could swear that they were moving. Tiny hands dropped from tiny mouths, exposing tiny glittering teeth. They seemed to be looking directly at him. He shook his head. This place; the darkness and the silence was getting to him. The silence and The Silences. What was going on? The atmosphere was making him hallucinate, imagine stuff that wasn't there. Shaking his head again, he did what he did best. Action, not emotion.

Crouching down, he used a small flashlight to examine the alarm system on the display case. It was simple enough, if the glass was broken or the cabinet moved then an audible alarm would sound in the room and a silent alarm would sound in the central security area of the museum. Easy enough to breach, it was intended to foil a daytime visitor, stealing on impulse, not some-one who came at night. He checked his watch, he was on schedule; the security patrol was still forty minutes out. Plenty of time. He tried his best to ignore the pain in his head, focusing on the job in hand. He glanced up at the cabinet, now at face level as he worked on the electrics of the alarm. Three tiny faces stared back at him. He fell backwards, his flashlight spinning off into the darkness, its light extinguished as the delicate bulb broke on impact. He managed not to scream, but it was close. Very close. What the hell was happening to him? His head was splitting open with pain, the endless silence ripping through his skull. Screw this, he decided. Something is wrong, I'm getting out of here. I don't need the money that much. He fought to stifle his panic and stood, ready to head back the way he had come. That rich collector could steal these vile things himself. He turned to leave, but some instinct drove him to turn once more to look at the figures. They were staring at him, their gaze capturing him, binding him. And then…then they spoke. There wasn't even enough time for him to scream.

The security guard was a bored man of some forty-five years old. He'd been doing this job for about two years; it suited his sluggish nature. Entering the European room, his flashlight examined the dark nooks and crannies. Apparently, he thought to himself, the museum authorities considered that this garbage was worth protecting. Not him though, it wasn't as if there were diamonds or gold on show, just some mouldy old pottery and statues. They were only valuable because they were old and some professor somewhere said that they were. He wouldn't buy any of it. His foot bumped something on the floor. He focused the beam of his flashlight to see what it was. It was a wee broken flashlight. Strange. Picking it up, he looked round the room, seeking for anything amiss. Nothing, everything was normal. Must have been dropped by a visitor. His own, powerful flashlight picked out the latest acquisition by the museum, those three little pottery figures. They were still there, in their display cabinet, all lined up, all with their little pottery hands firmly clamped over their little pottery mouths. He shivered. Those little figures gave him the creeps. Rubbing his forehead to try to dispel the beginnings of headache, he moved on towards the next room, whistling to break the silence that seemed to hang heavy over the museum.

Harrison climbed out of the car and lit another cigarette. He took one long drag from it to clear his lungs then he moved towards the building. His colleague, Jenkins, moved in beside him.

"He should still be asleep."

"Just like me then," grumbled Jenkins. He was still new to the job.

"Once you've done a few years you'll realise the best time to call on a suspect is while he's still asleep. That way you can arrest them before they know what's happening."

"I suppose so."

They reached the door of the building and Harrison tried the handle. Locked.

"Too early. We'll have to get the manager to open it. Press his call-button," said Harrison.

Jenkins leant forward to press the gold coloured knob that would wake the manager of the apartment building, whilst

Harrison turned round to look at the street behind them. The morning sun, just reaching over the rooftops of the city, cast a yellow glow across the road. The street's shops and businesses weren't open yet and there was a sense of quiet and calm. Harrison started to turn back when he caught sight of a solitary figure. It caught his attention because there was no-one else around. It was a tall man, standing about three or four streets down from them. It struck Harrison as odd that the man was just standing and staring. He wasn't opening up a shop or bustling off to work, just standing and staring directly at him. Harrison shivered, despite the warmth of the rising sun and turned to Jenkins.

"Jenkins, do you see that man down the road from us? Doesn't it seem odd to you that he's just standing there and staring at us."

Jenkins turned to look.

"What man? There isn't anybody there. It's too early."

"Open your eyes, mate. He's standing just down there..."

Harrison's voice trailed off as he looked back down the road. There was no longer any figure in sight.

"That's weird. He was there a minute ago."

Jenkins shrugged.

"Probably some bloke on his way to work."

"Yeah," replied Harrison unconvinced. There had been something about that figure. Something, but he didn't know what. It was definitely strange. His thoughts were interrupted by the arrival of the building manager, grumbling and cursing.

Harrison quickly forgot about the man. The daily hassle and grind drove the memory from his mind. The arrest had gone well; they had caught the suspect in possession of two kilos of cocaine, but there was other work to do. More of the usual rapes, murders and assaults that lay scattered throughout the day. By the time their shift was over at seven that evening the event was gone from his mind. Harrison buttoned up his coat against the cold night and lit his thirtieth cigarette of the day. By the time he went to bed he would have smoked nearly forty. He knew it was a rotten, stinking habit but he couldn't shake it off. The new dynamic millennium wasn't suited to smokers and he felt like an unhealthy pariah, trying to ignore dirty looks and barbed comments from those more health conscious than himself. Saying goodnight to Jenkins and the desk-sergeant, he headed towards the underground.

The night was sharp and clear. The bustle of the rush hour had just finished. The underground was about two streets from the police station and he covered the distance in about ten minutes. Thirty years on the force, with eight of them spent as a detective. Two more years then he could retire. He shut that thought out. Since Maisy had died he didn't want to think about it. When she was still alive they had planned what they would do together once he left the force. But now there was nothing. Nothing. She had left him too young, a victim of a drunk driver.

Harrison lit up again, knowing that he wouldn't have enough time to smoke it all before he got to the station. He coughed, the damp of the night getting to his chest. What a life.

He paused briefly to take a last drag before entering the underground station. He moved to toss the butt away. Suddenly he froze. There. Directly in front of him. The man. The one from that morning. Harrison was absolutely sure. It was the same man. Standing and staring directly at him. He was closer this time, about two hundred yards away, but Harrison still couldn't make out his features. He moved forward, towards the figure, but a crowd of tourists interrupted his stride. It took him a moment or two to clear the gaggle, pushing his way through brusquely. He was too late, the figure was gone.

He rushed to the spot where the man had stood. His nerves were jangling. There was no sign of him. He grabbed a young woman, standing at the edge of the pavement.

"Did you see that man?"

The girl squeaked in protest.

"Are you crazy? There was no-one here."

An older woman, attracted by the noise, ran across.

"What you doing to my friend? Leave her alone!"

"Get lost. I just want to talk to her."

Harrison pulled the young woman closer.

"That man. The one that was here about a minute ago. Did you see where he went?"

She looked at him, bewildered.

"I was alone. There was nobody else here."

"Tell me! He was just beside you."

"I'm telling the truth. There was no-one else."

Her eyes were scared. Scared of him. Harrison dropped her arm in disgust. He headed into the station.

The train was crowded but Harrison barely noticed. He was lost in thought. The same man twice in one day. Coincidence? After thirty years on the force Harrison didn't believe in coincidences. Something was happening. He lit up, ignoring the no smoking rule and the disgusted glances from his fellow passengers. It was to calm his nerves more than anything. He was more shaken than he cared to admit. It bothered him. He wasn't scared of much. In his time he had faced down robbers and murderers without too many sleepless nights. But this had shaken him. And it was nothing. Just a man. Staring. Just a man.

He coughed, deeply and painfully. Taking a drag cleared it. He stubbed his butt out on the floor of the train, knowing that he wouldn't be able to finish it; his chest was too tight.

His flat was dark and cold. Hanging his coat up, he put the lights and heating on. He double-locked the front door and, unusually, checked all the window locks. He was still shaken. He had a stiff shot of whisky and another cigarette then went straight to bed without eating. Sleep immediately came to him.

Dark sad eyes, burning red. Staring at him. Only a dream, but enough to wake him. The flat was in darkness. The bedside clock read 2 a.m. There was something wrong. Wide-eyed and alert, with no trace of sleepiness, he moved his head to look round his bedroom. Nothing. He rose.

The flat was empty. He went over it twice, but it was definitely empty. He scratched his head. His instincts couldn't have been wrong. He had been a police officer long enough to trust them. An unknown urge made him go to the window. The street below was empty, except for one thing. A tall figure, standing and staring. Him. Again. Harrison was immediately furious. He hurtled from his flat, rushing blindly. He would get the man this time.

The front door to the apartment block was locked. It took Harrison a moment or two to unlock it. The street outside was empty by the time he got there.

"Damn, damn!"

He was still furious. Not scared or shaken anymore; just down-right pissed off. A passing police car eye-balled him, but didn't stop. He headed back inside. Half-way there his chest constricted suddenly, doubling him up with another coughing fit. It soon passed, but his chest ached with a dull throb. He needed a cigarette badly, but he chose not to have one, and instead went back to bed.

When the alarm woke him at 6 a.m. his eyes were glued together with sleep and his head was heavy. He rubbed his eyes open. Eventually they responded. He felt really rough and he had to cough to clear his lungs before he could breathe properly.

"I'm too old to be running around at 2 a.m."

The shower finished the job of waking him, and by the time he'd had breakfast and another cigarette he felt alive again. But still annoyed. He was going to have to do something. Whoever was tailing him had to have a reason. He would ask around. Find out who was after him.

Somebody was bound to know. He headed for work.

The street outside his flat was bustling. He was later going to work than he had been the previous morning and the rush-hour was at its peak. He checked the street carefully, scanning it for signs of the figure. There was no sign of him. Harrison bent his head to light a cigarette. A voice spoke right beside him. A whisper.

"One more towards the grave, Mr. Harrison."

Harrison whirled round. It was him; the one who had been following him. Harrison stared at him, incredulous. The figure standing calmly right in front of him was dark. Not dark-skinned or dark-clothed, but *dark*. Real blackness. All Harrison could see was burning red eyes set in a fathomless face. Harrison's fury dissipated and his curses froze on his lips.

"What the hell?"

A female passer-by shot him a sideways look. The woman's eyes betrayed her thoughts; another nut in a city full of them.

"I wouldn't shout if I were you, Mr. Harrison. You look crazy. You see, nobody can see me except you."

"You're the crazy one. I'm taking you in, you bastard. Conspiracy. Give me your hands."

Acting like a policeman helped Harrison ignore the truth of what was in front of him. He knew it wasn't human, but he simply couldn't admit it. He automatically pulled the 'cuffs from his pocket, but his hand was suddenly twisted into a rigid claw by a painful spasm in his arm. Unable to keep his grip on the 'cuffs, they dropped to the ground. A larger bolt of pain shot through his entire left side, forcing his body to bend double. The man beside him looked on calmly as ever.

"That's the first seizure. It'll be over soon."

Harrison looked up at the man, his face in a rictus of pain.

"What are you doing to me?"

"Nothing. That's what's doing it, or rather that's what's done it."

The figure beside him pointed to the cigarette still dangling in Harrison's hand.

"What do you mean?"

"You've looked forward to death since your wife died. Now it's here; *I'm* here. I've come for you. You can finally relax and enjoy it. You see, after all this time, you've finally managed to kill yourself."

Harrison staggered forward, another blast of pain ripping through his body. He collapsed to his knees. Coughing violently, he tasted blood in his mouth. His eyes started to darken. People passing finally noticed his dilemma and came forward to help. Harrison didn't see them. He reached out to touch the figure in front of him.

"Help me. Please."

The man took his hand.

"Let's go," the dark man said, and he smiled a red-rimmed smile. Harrison went.

The view down into the valley from the mountainside was spectacular, there was no other word to describe it. Carl and Susan gazed down at the vision before them. Susan spoke, gushing.

"It's so wonderful. So spiritual, so enlightening!"

Carl nodded, focused less on the dramatic scenery and more on how exactly he was meant to pay for this trip-of-a-lifetime to the Himalayas. He was also still wondering how Susan, a long-time friend, had persuaded him to pay for the entire holiday for both of them. Amongst all the wonder and spirituality of this part of the world, he had pause to reflect that he was, as his friends had told him on many occasions, firmly and permanently in the friend zone. He checked his watch.

"We should head up to the lodge. It's still about five miles to go."

She nodded, still ecstatic about the view.

They were on a trekking holiday in Nepal. Ten days of unescorted hiking, with nightly accommodation and food provided. They travelled light, most of their gear was transported by vehicle so that it would be waiting for them at their next overnight stop.

The weather was perfect. The valleys below them were clear of snow. Carl could make out tiny figures busy in the fields. Dust clouds marked the passage of vehicles on the dirt roads. Above them, the mountain peaks that surrounded them were dazzling with snow and ice. It felt a million miles away from his normal suburban life.

They were scheduled to stay that night in one of the numerous little villages that sat amongst the foothills. Tomorrow they were heading higher towards one of the base camps near Everest. That was going to be the climax of their trip; not that they were climbing the peak itself, but merely to be camping near it was pretty impressive. Susan was looking forward to the opportunity to meditate near the world's tallest peak. Carl was looking forward to stopping walking. It was only a ten day trip, but already, on day five, he was knackered and chaffed in places he didn't realise he could get chaffed.

After a couple of hours of hard walking they entered the village where they were scheduled to stay for the night. Carl was puffing away, he wasn't as fit as Susan and the increase in altitude was affecting him. He was ready for a rest.

The village was typical of the mountain villages in the region, a scruffy, run-down collection of buildings scattered near the road-side. Prayer flags and bunting brought colour to the dull brown of the buildings. The village was busy with people going about their business, or merely sitting outside smoking and drinking tea. Various scruffy dogs and chickens wandered freely, somehow managing to avoid the traffic rolling through. It had the feel of a frontier town, one that might simply disappear overnight if fortunes changed. Susan checked her phone.

"The lodge is on the other side of the village, just outside."

"Okay, I'm dying to get my boots off and grab a shower."

It only took another five minutes to get to the lodge. It was a neater building than the others in the village, built to cater for the demanding western tourists who saturated the region throughout the year. The smiling owner showed them to their shared room, which was clean and neat. Carl slumped gratefully onto the bed, thankful for the comfort it provided. Their luggage had already arrived and Susan was fussing around with it, making sure everything was just right. Grabbing a towel, he opted to shower first.

In the shower, he had pause to think. He found that when he was away from home, whether that be for business or pleasure, he became more introverted, spending long hours thinking about himself and his life. Over the last few days of this, his first trip to the Himalayas, Carl had become painfully aware that the locals clearly viewed the over-dressed, plump foreigners with some bemusement. Tourists, like him, came in their thousands to seek experience, enlightenment and solace in a mountainous region on the far side of the world. Some even found death in the mountains, especially on Everest; most who died on that mountain stayed on that mountain, with the queues of would-be mountaineers shuffling past their corpses on the way to the summit. Carl had pause to consider how odd that scenario was. A conveyor belt of rich, over-privileged tourists from the first world, so hell-bent on conquering the world's highest peak that they would abandon their fellows on the mountain or walk past dying human beings. And what was it all for? Nothing more important than simple bragging rights. The Nepalese must think them all crazy.

Exiting the shower, he suggested to Susan that they take a stroll to see the village before their evening meal. She agreed.

As they strolled, they walked past homes, shops and the small temples and shrines so commonly seen in the region. As they passed one of these small temples, they heard the distinct whimpering of a young child from within. Susan, her sense of social justice as keen as ever, slowed and then stopped.

"Carl, I don't like the sound of that."

"Well, I'm sure it's nothing to do with us, so let's just keep walking."

She clutched his arm.

"No, let's go in. I want to see what is going on."

Carl followed her, mindful of her forceful, sometimes abrasive personality and aware that if any trouble developed he would be the one getting punched.

The inside of the temple was tiny, no more than five feet wide, ten feet long and about eight feet high. It was dim inside, the only light coming from sputtering candles. Incense burned in various parts of the room, the smoke obscuring the view. Carl could see that there was a shrine at the far end of the room. A statue of an elephant, draped in colourful flower garlands. Plates with what presumably were offerings had been placed on the floor. Susan was already standing by the shrine when Carl entered. She gestured to him.

"Look at this, Carl. Look at this outrage!"

Carl joined her and looked. On the floor lay a small child, no more than five or six years old. He was crouched in a foetal position under the indifferent eyes of the elephant statue. Dressed in rags, his skin was covered in sores and filth. Carl spoke.

"He must have been abandoned here. How terrible."

Carl was actually pretty shocked by the sight. The child was shuffling and whining, his thin arms rubbing his face as his tears tracked clean marks through the dirt. Carl had seen some shocking amounts of poverty and deprivation during this trip, but this was by far the worst.

"What should we do?" he asked.

"Well, we need to contact the authorities. Carl, pick him up."

Carl, sympathetic as he was, blanched at the thought of touching the filthy child. Susan sensed his hesitation and frowned.

"Don't be so silly! Just pick the child up! For goodness sake, Carl, do I have to do everything?"

There was a gentle cough from behind them and a voice spoke.

"My master says, please do not touch the child."

Carl and Susan turned towards the entrance to see two short figures standing on the threshold. One was a young man, around twenty years old, dressed in jeans and a t-shirt. His companion was an elderly man, dressed in a long flowing robe. The old man bowed and said something in the local dialect. The younger man nodded.

"My master says that you are not the first to see this boy, but you must leave him alone and you must leave the temple."

Carl could feel Susan tense up.

"This child is in a very bad way, you understand?"

Her voice grew shriller, a sure sign that she was furious. The old man nodded, as if he understood what she said, but then he spoke again in the same dialect. The young man spoke.

"My master asks if you want some tea. Please."

"Yes, thank you."

Carl had interjected before Susan could answer. He didn't want to cause any problems with the locals and he was suddenly aware that they were in a potentially vulnerable situation. He didn't think there would be any violence, but he didn't want any unpleasantness to mar his trip. He placed his hand on hers to mollify her. She stiffened then relaxed. The young man gestured with a smile. Carl and Susan stepped out of the temple into the early evening sun.

The tea was served to them as they sat at a rough wooden table in the only café in town. A few disinterested villagers sat nearby smoking and drinking tea or coffee. The four people sat round sipping their tea. No-one spoke for a few moments, then the old man began to speak. The young man translated.

"My master says that you have seen the child and that you must be shocked by such a sight."

Carl and Susan nodded.

"My master says that you must not interfere or move the child. The child is a...fixed point. That is the closest English term to the word in our language."

"A fixed point?" asked Susan, with disgust in her voice. The old man nodded and spoke in fractured English.

"Yes. Fixed point. Good."

He nodded, smiling. The young man said something to the old man in the quick-fire language of the region. The old man nodded. The young man spoke.

"My master has given me permission to speak freely, so that you understand. In our religion we believe that there are certain children who are selected by our gods to bear the burden of sin for all humanity. This child, the one in the temple, is such a creature. He looks young, but he is more ancient than anyone living in the village. He was born to absorb our sin, to be punished instead of us. It is…his role. He was chosen for this. The people go to the temple to pray, confess and bring offerings. He lies in that temple, absorbing the darkness of the world. Soon, his time will be over and he will ascend to heaven, to be revered as a god. Without him, and those like him, the earth would descend into darkness, as the burden of our sin destroys us."

Susan stared in shock.

"You mean to tell me that this child is allowed just to lie in that temple in his own filth, whilst you...you people believe that this is the right way to behave. It is barbaric!"

The young man spread his hands.

"It is not just our belief. It is the truth. He is the eater of sins. He was born for this role. You must leave him alone. He must stay in the temple, absorbing the sins of the world."

Susan just stared at the two men, her face showing the obvious disgust that she felt. She spoke.

"Well, we will have to see about that."

The two locals spoke briefly in their own language, then the younger man spoke again.

"Please, do not do anything to interfere."

Susan stood up.

"I will do what I think is best."

Later in the room, Carl sat next to Susan on the bed.

"I think the best thing to do is wait until we get back to Kathmandu and then contact the authorities," said Carl.

"They won't do anything. And it might be too late by then. That child is at death's door. I can't stand to think that here we are, well fed and sleeping in comfortable beds, when just a few feet away that poor little boy is starving and suffering."

"Look, this is a poor country. There are children suffering everywhere. Why worry about just one? I think we should just let some-one know when we get back to Kathmandu. One of the aid agencies, perhaps."

Susan looked at him, her jaw firm and set. Carl spoke, in a pleading tone.

"Now, can we just go to bed? I'm tired and we have a long day tomorrow."

Carl woke the next morning to silence. Normally Susan rose before him and the noise of her getting dressed woke him. On this morning, it was the silence that did the job. He looked over to her bed. It was empty and her gear was gone.

"Oh no, Susan. What have you done?"

He rose and dressed quickly, worried about what he was going to find outside. Once dressed, he headed out into the village. He knew where to go. The small temple was in turmoil, with a large group of villagers milling around outside. Carl spotted the young man from the day before. Their eyes locked and the young man came running over to Carl.

"What have you done with him?"

"Who?" answered Carl, but he already knew the answer.

"The child. He is gone."

"I haven't done anything with him. I've just woken up."

"Then your friend must have taken him."

Carl knew that statement to be true. That's exactly what she had done. He could even imagine the scenario. Dressing and packing quietly in the dead of the night, whilst Carl lay snoring. Sneaking out of the lodge and into the temple. Quelling her revulsion for long enough to pick the emaciated child up, then heading down the mountain to the next village to pick up a taxi. She'd be well on her way to Kathmandu by now. Thanks Susan, he thought to himself, thanks for leaving me to pick up the pieces. He spoke to the young man.

"I didn't know what she was going to do. She must have left in the middle of the night."

The young man nodded, clearly believing him.

"What are you going to do now?" asked Carl, fearing the worst. The young man gave a grim smile.

"Nothing, it is already too late. So many of you foreigners have come here and have seen the child. But only your friend was arrogant enough to think that we were lying to her. What are we going to do? What can we do, Englishman? What can we do, when we were telling you the truth? Without that child, that fixed point to absorb our sins, the darkness is coming."

He pointed at the sky. Carl looked up. The young man had been right all along; the sun, without any fuss or drama, was going out.

There were two voices on the recording, one suave and cultured, the other a bit rougher.

"A tape machine, don't see many of them anymore," said the rougher voice.

"We prefer them to digital. Less easy to hack into," answered the more cultured voice. The cultured voice continued.

"Tell me again, this amazing story of yours."

"Again?"

"Again."

There was a sigh.

"Okay. Again."

A glass clinked as someone took a drink.

"It all happened in June. Klablooie! Atomic war, who would have thought it? Damn terrorists. Middle East, that's where it started, but it didn't stop there. Spread like butter. Lots of countries involved, even those that weren't got hit."

"Where were you at this time?"

"At home, where else? Luckily we lived in the countryside, so we missed the blasts that hit the cities. But the damage was terrific and boy, the fallout…"

"How did you survive the next few months?"

"Barely, I tell you. Who prepares for a nuclear war in this day and age? Everyone thought that threat was gone, over since the nineteen eighties. But those terrorists had other ideas, didn't they? Set a few bombs off in select locations. Then it just escalated, governments firing missiles at each other, not even bothering to find out who fired first.

We hunkered down in our basement, me and the wife. We were joined by four others; John and Delores from the farm across the road, Erika from next door and Kal from a few houses up. Erika's husband Rob was away that day, we never saw him again. Same with Kal's wife Cathy. I think she was at work or something.

Just after the bombs dropped, we raided the nearest supermarket and then just settled down, hoping to get rescued. I tell you, buddy, it got real cold, real fast. Even though it was June when it all hit, temperatures dropped to well below freezing real quick. Luckily, we had wood stores left over from the previous winter and a fireplace in the basement. We did okay. For a while."

"So what happened then?"

"Well, things started to go bad after a while. John went outside and cut himself on barbed wire. He died two weeks later of some horrible infection. We dumped him outside. Delores wasn't too unhappy, her and Kal had been getting close anyway. Then the water started to run low, which was pretty bad, but we managed to get some more from the well in the back garden. The food was the worst, we ran out pretty quick. It was still bad outside, we knew that the air was radioactive, that the earth itself was poisoned. We had been more or less safe in the basement, but we had no more food. The only option was to go outside and raid some more supermarkets."

"And this was when this incident happened?"

"Yes. It was me and Kal that volunteered to go out. It happened on the way back from the supermarket. We hadn't got much, maybe enough cans for a few days. There must have been lots of other survivors in the town, the shelves were almost empty. My stomach was already rumbling and we was worried. How were we going to feed five people on a few crappy cans of meat? And then…"

"Then?"

"Well, then these guys appeared. Four of them. Straight away they looked out of place. They were clean for a start, all dressed in suits."

"So you claim that you met the President, the Vice-President, the Secretary of Defence and the Secretary of State of the United States on a rural road near your home."

"Yup, not that I was too bothered at the time. My mind was on other things."

"Like food?"

"Like food."

"Did they speak to you?"

"Yes, they did.   I remember it exactly.   They told us who they were and then they said that they had returned back to this time to once more lead the people into a brand new future. I thought it was strange that they used the word time and not place, but I figured it was just a slip."

"And how did you feel about them returning to govern once more?"

"Pretty riled, actually.   Here they were, all plump and well-fed, dressed in their sleek suits and here was us, a couple of scruffy scarecrows with our ribs poking through our skin. They looked smug, oily. And they were the ones who had pushed the button, after all. It was kinda all their fault."

"How did Kal react?"

"He was pretty annoyed too. He had the same feeling as me. Somehow these guys had caused the war and then avoided the consequences.   And then Kal had his idea."

"To eat them."

There was a pause on the tape, almost embarrassed.

"Yup, to eat them. We was hungry. You ever been really hungry, mister?"

"So, how did you find out about this so-called time machine?"

"Well, once we had them tied up in the basement, they tried to persuade us that they had avoided the war by going back in time, waiting for a few months then coming back to the present to continue to lead the country. They even told us where the machine was located, in the air force base a few miles north of the town."

"But you ate them anyway."

"Well, we didn't believe them of course, they were just trying to save their skins. A time machine? Bullplop, I say."

"But, you ate them anyway?" the voice repeated.

"Oh, sure. We ate them. Pretty tasty too."

"So when did you discover they had been telling the truth about the time machine?"

"Wasn't till a few weeks later. I'd had a row with Kal and my wife, so went out on my own to cool off. By that time, I wasn't worried about fallout no more. I remembered what those guys had said, so I went up to the base, just see what they were talking about. Just in case they hadn't been lying. They told us that it was a cubicle, like a porta potty on steroids in the middle of the runway and so it was. Just sitting there. I opened the door and went in."

"What did you see inside?"

"Just one lever."

"And you pulled it."

"Yup."

"And that was when you arrived here, three days ago. Right in the middle of the same air force base on high alert."

"Yup."

"You were lucky not to be shot, especially looking the way you do."

"I guess, but I am a citizen. I have rights."

"Indeed. So, is there anything else you want to add?"

"No."

"Okay, interview terminated, 13.45."

There was a pause.

"Okay, take him back to his cell."

The tape clicked off.

Later, after listening to the interview, the distinguished figure of the President of the United States leaned back in his chair.

"So, how does he know about Project Phoenix?"

The agent, the one who had conducted the interview answered.

"No idea, sir. His story is ludicrous."

"But the tests do show that he is suffering from mild radiation sickness."

"True."

"And we do have a time machine."

"True."

The President closed his eyes and went silent for a long time. Then he spoke.

"Bring us down from DEFCON 2 to DEFCON 5. Cancel the alerts in all air force and army bases. Get my counterparts on the phone. If it was terrorists who set off these devices, rather than *them*, then I don't want to make a mistake that will lead to war. Let's talk, not fight."

"Yes sir!"

The agent left the room. The President looked round the bare, stark interview room.

"It was a good idea to save us using the time-hop theory, but I really don't want to end up serving the people in *that* way."

I

He sat at the dining room table, pretending to scan the list in front of him. A pencil in his hand was poised, ready to mark off the course he was looking for when he found it. Wendy passed by and glanced down.

"You and your silly courses. What is it going to be this time?"

"I fancy car maintenance this year. It'll save garage bills."

"At least it'll do some good this time. What was it last year, wine appreciation? Grown men and women spending their evenings spitting out perfectly good wine."

He just smiled.

"It was fun and I learnt a lot. I now know what a good Medoc tastes like."

"As if we can afford one. Just make sure that whatever course you choose, it isn't too expensive."

"Yes, dear."

He continued looking down the list, scanning carefully. He saw the course he was actually looking for, listed beneath the courses on child-care. His pencil marked a careful cross beside the car maintenance course for beginners. Marking car maintenance was part of the charade, acted out for Wendy's benefit. He went on the same course, year in and year out. It was always Cooking for One. Always. How else could he indulge his secret little hobby of screwing around?

He folded up the flyer from the Adult Education Centre and placed it into his briefcase. He would phone from work, just to save a little money. And to avoid her finding out, his mind slyly coughed up. Well, he had to have some fun. She was crap in bed anyway. It was easier to find some youngish spinster or single mum on the Cooking for One course, chat her up and then bed her. You didn't have to try to please them on a one night stand.

He always played the role of 'single guy, just moved into the area and learning to cook'. After all, who else but happily single people would go on a Cooking for One course? It was almost too simple, like shooting targets at a fairground; some of them were absolutely gagging to be chatted up and bedded. He sometimes screwed an ugly one just to see the pathetic gratitude on their piggy faces. Some of them even gave up their virginity to him, just because he told them that he loved them. He would never see them again, of course, and that was a real pain. After he had them he couldn't exactly go back on the course and face them again. The worst year was when he had pulled on the very first night of the course, screwed her in the back of his car then had to spend every Tuesday for the rest of the ten week course drifting round pubs without drinking, going to the cinema by himself or simply driving around to while away the hours. Still, hassle or not, it was the buzz that drove him back, year after year.

There was always the chance that someone he knew would be studying at the same centre, on some course or other, and that they would bump into each other. In fact, it had already happened a couple of times, but they had just been acquaintances and it had been easy to brush them off. It wasn't an issue. Wendy knew that he was there, it was just the course he was taking that was different. His main worry was that the staff at the centre would realise that this one man kept coming back on the same course, year after year. He was sure that they couldn't do anything about it, he had paid his money after all, but it would look suspicious and it might cause him some embarrassment if they questioned him. So, every time he took a different name.

He phoned the centre to register on the course. There were still places available according to the woman on the other end of the phone. He casually asked who was teaching it. The woman mentioned some female's name but it didn't ring a bell in his mind. A different one to last time. Good, she wouldn't know him from Adam. The same instructor had been teaching the course for the last three years and he suspected that she had guessed what he was up to when he kept turning up. Still, that sort of thing just added to the excitement. The woman on the other end of the phone asked his name. He said the first word that popped into his mind.

"Adam...," his eyes drifted across his desk to his computer. "Adam Macintosh."

II

The first night of the course was a Tuesday as usual. It was wet and miserable, as befitted an October evening. He made sure that he had no late meetings at work and tried to get home as early as possible. Jenkins kept him talking in the corridor for an extra fifteen minutes and he had to speed to get home by six. The man was an idiot! Always whining about his job, his home, his family. Why the hell didn't he just divorce his wife and move? It was baffling.

After a quick meal, he showered and dressed in casual stuff. He didn't want to dress up too much, that would be too obvious, but nor did he want to be too scruffy. Clothes were one of the first things that a woman noticed about a man. He had read that in Wendy's Cosmopolitan. He headed for the door.

"I'm off, pet. See you later."

"Don't get too mucky."

What? He almost spoke the word before he clicked where he was meant to be going. Car maintenance.

"I won't, dear. I'm sure I'm won't be doing anything too dirty tonight." He smiled at his own joke.

He parked in his usual part of the car park and walked into the building, feeling its familiarity settle round him. He changed from married man to single male as he entered through the portals of the centre. He was now Adam Macintosh, designer and hopeless cook.

The centre was an old secondary school, closed when a new comprehensive had been built two miles down the road. The old school had been surplus to requirements and had been converted into an Adult Education Centre.

The course was run in a room that had once been a classroom for Home Economics. It had about twenty gas cookers and beside them, a single desk which doubled as a work surface. At the front there was the standard teacher's desk and blackboard. Being back in a school, any school, made him feel funny every time. Some things never got out of your system.

There were about ten people in the room when he arrived. He quickly scanned them, checking to make sure that he didn't know anyone. This was the point when he was at his most paranoid, at the moment of no return. Thoughts of one of Wendy's friends, or even worse, one of his ex-one night-stands appearing in the classroom haunted him. But it hadn't happened yet and it didn't happen then. There was nothing but a sea of unfamiliar faces in front of him. There were six women and four men. Three of the women were definite no-no's. Total dogs, not even he would touch them. The other three were reasonable, one was a bit too old, but she would do in a pinch. Of the men there was one definite poof, Cooking for One was popular with that type too, and the other three weren't going to be any competition. No, he was definitely top cock in this class.

The instructor hadn't arrived yet and he took the time to choose himself a good position. There was no point, for example, being wedged between the poof and one of the dogs. No, he had to get near to the women that were worth screwing. He spotted a free desk at the far end of the room, near the windows. It sat beside one of the decent women. It was a little bit isolated from the rest of the class, but that was all the better. He wouldn't get interrupted with small talk and if he didn't get involved with the group then nobody would remember his face. Well, no-one except the one he screwed. She would definitely remember him.

He walked to the desk, smiling at people as he passed. They smiled nervously back. The first night was always awkward and he prided himself on being the most sociable person in the group. It was a good way to break the ice and he had read that women were always attracted to confident men.

He surveyed the items on his desk, it was the same for every first class. A basic chicken casserole type-thing. A couple of scabby chicken bits and a few mangy vegetables were laid out on the table. Once it was cooked they were expected to take it home, but of course he couldn't. He didn't even eat it, normally throwing it over the nearest hedge on his way home.

He put his oven on, in preparation for the class. The instructor still hadn't arrived. He turned to the woman next to him and spoke.

"Typical of this place, we pay our money and the instructor is late!"

He smiled ingratiatingly at her, trying not to show too many teeth. She smiled back.

"Adam Macintosh is the name. I'm new in town and I've decided it's about time I learnt to cook. Normally I'm a restaurant man; that is when I get time to eat! My life is all go, go, go!"

"What do you do to be so busy?"

"Oh, I'm a freelance web designer. You know, picking up work here and there. It's such a busy life-style."

"I thought that web designers were normally young."

Screw you, he thought to himself. You won't be getting it from me tonight. He mentally struck her off his list of possibilities. Two to go.

"Well, some of the better known web designers are young, I suppose, but it takes experience as well, you know. I've been at it since the early nineties. Got a fairly solid reputation. These young guys can't stand the pace, they blow themselves out too quickly. Most laypeople don't know that."

"Well, I do actually. My partner is a web designer too. Works for Ernest and Ross, the advertising agency in London. Do you know them?"

Of course he didn't know them. He knew absolutely nothing about web designing, having picked up his imaginary career from Cosmopolitan.

"I'm not sure," he said, trying to sound casual.

"Well, my partner says that they're one of the best known companies in the UK.

As a designer I thought you would have heard of them."

He desperately tried not to get into an argument, but he just couldn't help himself.

"Well, he would say that, he does work for them."

The woman glared at him.

"She, actually."

It took him a moment to realise what she'd just said. Then it dawned. It was pretty apparent that the woman had known the shock value. It blew his argument, he couldn't think of anything to say.

"Oh, right."

He turned away and started to study the recipe card, trying to ignore the smug look on the woman's face. If she had been a bloke, he would have thumped her, a tiny macho voice shouted from deep inside him.

III

It was another ten minutes before the instructor turned up. One of the men had already left in disgust, making some unintelligible comment to the air. The whole class turned round when the door opened.

She was gorgeous. All thoughts of trying to pull one of his classmates went out the window. For the first time in his illustrious career as an adulterer, he had decided to go for the instructor.

She wasn't particularly tall, probably only 5'3" or 5'4". She was slim. Her hips weren't too big and her dark hair tumbling over her shoulders accentuated the dark beauty of her face. She was altogether gorgeous.

She walked to the front of the class, with some embarrassment. Dumping her bag on the front desk, she removed her jacket and slung it over the chair behind her. She spoke to the class.

"Hello everybody. Sorry for being late. My bus was delayed by the rush hour. My name is Alison and I'll be taking you all for this course in Cooking for One. I'm sure that I'll get to know all your names as we go along. Let's get started. Can you please turn to the recipe sheets in front of you?"

The class continued but he paid little attention to what was going on. He was no longer interested in anybody but Alison. She was his challenge for this session. He would either get her or have no-one, but he wasn't prepared to lose. She didn't have a wedding ring; okay, that didn't mean much in this day and age, but at least she might not be married. At least, she didn't want to tell people that she was married, which amounted to the same thing in his eyes.

He managed to make eye contact with her on a number of occasions and she smiled back at him when her eyes met his. His heart leapt in anticipation. He was getting somewhere. His hopes started to rise.

He already had his excuse to chat her up. You had to be sharp in this game. She had mentioned the bus. No car. He would play the gallant gentleman, going her way. No matter where she lived, he would be going her way. Then he would get *his* way.

He lifted his hand to attract her attention. She smiled and walked across to him.

"What's the matter," she glanced at the name badge on his chest. "Adam."

"I can't get the hang of it. I'm not very good at this."

His tone reflected confusion and bewilderment. It was meant to convey vulnerability to her. Perhaps he over-played it, because the lesbian glared at him. Maybe she fancied teacher as well. Well, he would get her and prove that a man was better.

"What don't you understand?"

"Um...why do we have to brown the chicken if it's going to be cooked anyway?"

He made a mental note to think of a question before he put his hand up next time. She smiled, giving him a long, steady look, almost as if she could read his mind and his intentions.

"Good question. It's to seal in the juices so that the meat remain tender. I do like nice tender meat."

She over-emphasised the word 'meat' and stared directly into his eyes, with a slight smile playing round her lips. This was it! The woman was gagging for it and he was the man to give it to her. He had fantasised about meeting a woman like her ever since he started coming to Cooking for One. A woman who would be happy to play the part of the seducer. Now it was happening. He had to let her know he was interested but not too keen. He tried to say something smart and sexy.

"Oh, yes. I like meat. Especially a nice a bit of breast. Mind you, a nice leg satisfies me as well," he replied, trying unsuccessfully to stop his voice squeaking.

"We'll have to see what we can do. You seem to be a keen student. Perhaps you'd like to have some extra...tuition. There is time after the class tonight, if you want?"

"I'd love to. I definitely would like some extra instruction."

His voice again rose to a boyish squeak at the end of the sentence. She didn't seem to notice. Or care.

"Good."

She moved away and the lesbian next to him glared again. Tough crap, he thought gloatingly, I've pulled her, not you. He smiled sweetly back and the woman turned away in disgust.

IV

The class had finished and the people were packing up their efforts into casserole dishes or plastic bowls. One by one they left the room, leaving only him, Alison and the lesbian. Alison was tidying up her desk. The lesbian finished and walked to the front desk, as she pulled on her jacket.

"I heard you say that you got the bus here tonight. Do you want a lift home?"

His heart fell.

"No thanks. Adam and I are going to do a bit more work."

His heart jumped up again.   Jill shrugged, glared at him once more and then left. They were alone. Alison walked up to him, and put her hand on his bare arm.

"Take me home."

V

"Where do you live?" he asked once they were in the car.

"I'll direct you. It's hard to find."

"Okay."

He managed to stifle the tremble in his voice. He couldn't believe his luck, he had been pulled on the first night and by an absolute stunner. He just couldn't believe his luck.

"Left here."

He turned the wheel and her hand brushed against him. He bit his lip.

"Right, at the corner."

He turned right.

"You can stop here."

He did so, quickly. They got out the car and he looked round. They were in a part of town that he didn't recognise. He hoped that he could get home alright. She lived on a street of Edwardian townhouses, mostly converted into apartments. It looked like a nice part of town, it had character and was far nicer than the new-build estate that he and Wendy lived on. She had good taste; well, you could tell that from the men she liked.

He followed her up to a doorway, which stood at the top of about four or five steps. They didn't speak, but her hand sought his and held it tight. They entered the building and climbed the stairs to the first floor. She was in front of him and he watched her buttocks move in the trousers that she was wearing. It was a beautiful sight. She stopped outside a varnished wooden door and turned round. Her eyes were bright and her lips were moist. He realised that she was as excited as he was. She opened the door and motioned him to enter the flat. It was sparsely decorated, with a minimal amount of furniture.

"Go and sit in the lounge. I'll get ready."

He sat. After a few moments she entered the room, dressed the same as before but with her hands hidden behind her back. He was disappointed that she wasn't wearing some sort of sexy underwear. Still, maybe she was hiding something interesting.

"What sort of thing do you fancy?" he asked.

She walked forward and smiled. Her cheeks were red with excitement. She smiled and answered.

"I like my meat red and rare."

"You've come to the right place then, darling."

"I know," she said and brought her hands out from behind her back. That was when he saw the knife in her hand and, in the split second before he died, realised what she actually meant.

It was a warm October evening and the capital seemed full of life. Ira and Myra liked London. They were on their first visit to the city, staying in a small hotel in Kensington. They hadn't splashed out on five-star accommodation because they were on a tight budget, unlike some people who acted like typical loud, brash and rich American tourists. In other words, they weren't like that terrible Henderson couple who they had met that day in the British Museum. They had been so common. Rich, but common. He had made his money in pork or something. She had been the archetypal hideous American housewife, all costume jewellery, bleach blonde hair and polyester yoga pants. They had nothing in common with them at all. Dreadful people!

Even the thought of them made Myra shiver, as she pulled on her cardigan. Despite the balmy evening, it was possible that it would get cold later and at her age she was more affected by the cold than she had been twenty years before.

"Weren't they just terrible?"

"Who, dear?" asked Ira, who was sitting on the small bed, in the small bedroom, tying his shoe-laces.

"Those awful people in that lovely museum today. They spoilt the whole Egyptian section for me. That terrible woman, she never stopped talking."

"Don't upset yourself, dear, we can go back tomorrow. They won't be back. I'm sure that their type wouldn't go back to such a nice place."

"No way, they were far too common. Did you see the way they were dressed?"

She shivered again. Ira sighed. This would be it for the night. Moan, moan, moan and all about something which she could do nothing about. It had always been the same, all the way through their forty year marriage. She was far too polite to say anything at the time, but boy would she whine about it when they were alone. It had been exactly the same on their wedding night. She had sat on the end of their marriage bed and complained bitterly about his mother. Not a single thought for him and his needs. Just moan, moan, moan.

"What are you looking so miserable about?" she snapped.

"Nothing dear. Shall we go for our walk?"

The warm wind soothed Ira's mind as they started on their walk. It was way past dusk, but the sky still had a thin sliver of light down near the horizon, all reds and purples. It was beautiful against the jumbled skyline of the city and the darkness of the rest of sky. London wasn't like any other city; it was a city of layers, of mysteries, of a deep and long history. Even Ira, not the most imaginative person, could see that it was a city that had seen hate, love, war and peace over the millennia that it had been in existence. It was a place where you could be 'someone' or it could be a place for people to disappear. A place where all things were possible. A place of dreams, and of nightmares. A tune trickled through Ira's mind. Some British band singing a song called 'Waterloo Sunset'. Now he knew what they meant, what the writer had been feeling when he had penned those words. He wondered if Myra would consider watching the sunset from Waterloo one night, wherever it was, but quickly dumped the idea. She would have no idea what he was talking about.

They had been walking for about half an hour when Ira noticed that they were moving away from the busier, crowded streets into a quieter, more residential part of town. It felt as if they were moving into an older part of the city. An ancient part of the city, his mind corrected him for no particular reason. To Ira, it felt just a bit creepy, but he couldn't work out why. Maybe it was just the quiet amongst the bustle. At home quiet was the norm, here it was the exception. Ira spoke, interrupting the silence that they normally kept during their walks.

"Myra, don't you think we should be getting back? We don't want to get lost."

"You've got the A-Z, haven't you?"

"Well, yes...but."

She interrupted him.

"Then we'll be fine. If we get lost, we'll just get a cab."

"Okay, honey."

He hadn't seen a cab for at least five blocks, but he didn't bother trying to argue. It wasn't worth it. Myra was walking off the anger created by the Henderson couple and the best way to keep her from taking it out on him was simply to keep her moving.

There was no-one on the streets that they were walking on. The street-lights had already come on and they bathed the street in orange light, the gleam reflecting off the cars parked up for the night. Myra sped up, fuelled by her anger no doubt. He couldn't be bothered to keep up, knowing that she would eventually wait for him. He looked around, relishing the unfamiliarity of the scene despite his creepy feelings. The houses around him were big, some had four floors. They were old houses by the look of it, solid in their comfortable red-brick. The well-established gardens, with old trees and solid hedges, complimented the houses. Most of the dwellings were lit with warm yellow lights, which served to remind Ira of just how homesick he actually was. He could see people sitting in their houses, watching television or simply reading. He felt a pang of jealously. It had been Myra's idea to come on vacation, before they were both too old to enjoy it. He would rather have just stayed at home and played golf with his buddies, spending the holiday money on a really good set of clubs. He wondered what his friends were up to.

Suddenly from the darkness on his left hand side there jumped a short, terrifying figure. It screamed at him, baring fangs and claws. He felt his bladder go in shock and was aware of a warm wetness spreading down the front of his thankfully dark-coloured slacks.

It took him a full two or three seconds to realise that the figure in front of him was not some hideously deformed demon, but simply a child dressed up. Three or four similarly dressed figures followed the first one, all running up and down the street in front of Ira. They carried bags and jumped up and down in excitement. He suddenly remembered what day it was. The

31st of October. Trick-or-treaters had caused him to wet his pants. He laughed despite the dampness spreading rapidly across his trousers.

A larger figure loomed from the alleyway on his left, where the kids had come from. An adult, no doubt, supervising the kids. Ira smiled at the unseen person, who was still hidden in shadow. The adult moved under the streetlight and Ira saw it was a perfectly pleasant looking young woman. Hell, she was young enough to still be classed as a girl, only nineteen or twenty. Probably the kids' nanny, or something. She smiled at him and as she did so, she went from pleasant looking to downright beautiful.

"Hello. I hope that the brats didn't scare you. They've been doing that sort of thing all night. Frightful, aren't they?"

"Nope. It's good to see kids having fun."

He neglected to mention his pants. If it had been in America, he probably would have been phoning his lawyer. He preferred Britain.

"Well, it is Halloween. One night a year isn't too bad."

"It is nice," he replied, unable to think of anything else to say. His wet pants, now cold, were proving to be an unwelcome diversion. He prayed that she wouldn't notice.

"Gosh, you're American. Visiting London?"

"Yes, my wife and I are touring Europe. England is our last stop."

Just then, Myra came back to see what was keeping him. She had *that* face on.

"Hi Myra."

Myra ignored the girl standing with Ira and spoke directly to him. The children ran under her feet, nearly tripping her up.

"I waited for you at the top of the block. I knew that you would get into trouble."

"I'm not in trouble. I just passing some time with these good folk. They're trick-or-treating."

"That's nice. Let's go. We can't be out too late."

"Okay."

He turned to the girl who was standing silently beside him. The children chattered noisily around him. It was a beautiful sound. He touched the head of one of them and she raised her head and smiled an innocent smile at him. He couldn't help smiling back.

"Ira."

That was the first grumbled warning. It wouldn't be the last if he didn't obey her.

"Well, it was nice to meet you. Good luck with the rest of your trick-or-treating."

"Thanks very much. Enjoy your walk."

The girl smiled at him, with something approaching sympathy, but her eyes held something else in them. An invitation, perhaps, but to what? The smile was a secret, just for him. She seemed to be speaking to him, saying secret words. He wanted to ask her what she meant, what she wanted him to do because he didn't quite understand, but then Myra took his arm, breaking the spell, and they walked off together. A few yards down the road Myra dropped his arm. He turned to look back and he saw the girl still standing there, with the children still playing at her feet. What he wouldn't have given to go back to her and find out her secret.

They continued their walk, moving further into the residential area. Gradually, the traffic noises that had been ever present in the background faded and they found themselves walking in silence. After the episode with the girl, Ira was in no mood to speak to Myra and instead enjoyed the quiet. He had never considered himself to be particularly imaginative, but he knew that he hadn't been imagining what had happened with the girl. She had been saying something to him, something that he was sure Myra wasn't to know.

His pants had dried without Myra noticing. She never would have stopped about that one, no doubt bringing it up again and again at their barbeques back home. Her cronies would have loved that story.

He tried to keep note of the streets that they were walking on, but soon he realised that they were effectively lost. Somewhere in the distance he could hear noise, but he couldn't work out what it was. It wasn't traffic noise. He looked at his watch and realised that it was also starting to get late. It was nearly eleven o'clock. They had been out for more than three hours, but it hadn't felt like that. He would have sworn that they had only been walking for around an hour. He tried to think what time he had met the girl with the children, but he couldn't think. It hadn't seemed like five minutes ago, but surely kids that age weren't allowed to stay up that late in Britain?

As if in response to this thought, lights started to go out in the houses around them, as people settled down for the night. The memory of the warmth of the girl's gaze faded and his basic practicality returned. Ira started to feel a tiny bit worried.

"Myra, I think we should head back now."

She had obviously had the same thought.

"Where are we?"

"I don't rightly know, honey. I think we need to look at the A-Z. Let's stand beside one of those streetlights."

They huddled together under the streetlight and Ira pulled out the A-Z.

"What's the name of this street?"

"Crouchtown Market Alley," said Myra, squinting up at the street sign on the corner.

"C…Crouch…Crouchtown…um… no Crouchtown Market Alley. Sounds very Victorian, like it was taken from Dickens."

"What's the next street?" asked Myra, ignoring him. This wasn't the time for whimsy.

"Let's look."

As they walked to the next street Ira became aware that the noise he had earlier heard was getting louder. He could finally identify the sounds that he had heard. It was people laughing and shouting. Like a party, he thought. Ira felt jealous. He wished that he was having a good time, rather than wandering around lost in the dark. He wished he was having a good time with that girl he had bumped into. Myra, who had strode ahead again, stopped.

"It's called Tollhouse Towne Junction."

He looked in his book again.

"Nope. Nothing."

"Can't we just find our way back again? Retrace our steps."

"Well, honey, I can't remember which way we came. Can you?"

"Oh, Ira, you're useless."

"We could call a cab," suggested Ira.

"I haven't seen a call-box or a cab. Have you?"

Ira hadn't. They were in a residential area, after all.

"We could ask some-one."

"Who?"

"Well, we could ask at one of the houses."

He looked around, searching for a lit window. There were none. He checked his watch. Midnight. There was no way! It hadn't taken them an hour to check two street-names! He shook his watch, trying to force it to tell the real time. It still read midnight. Around them the merriment carried on, the sounds echoing off the walls. He distinctly heard a child's voice raised. There was a roar of laughter in response, which drowned out the child's sharp voice.

"We could head for that party. We wouldn't be disturbing them and I'm sure they'd help."

"What party? What the hell are you talking about, Ira?"

"The party. We can just follow the sound of the party."

"I can't hear anything."

"Myra, you must be getting deaf. Come on, or we're never going to get back to the hotel tonight."

He set off. She followed him, complaining. He turned left and right, trying to keep the noise of laughter and gaiety ahead of him. As he walked the houses changed, looking less like neat Edwardian or Victorian townhouses and more like ancient cottages and shacks with thatched roofs, but Ira barely noticed. He was amazed that a party was still going on, in this quiet suburb of London. It seemed incongruous at this time of night. He would have thought that the residents wouldn't have stood for such a noise so late at night. Didn't the British have laws about that sort of thing? Still, it didn't matter to him, as long as they could get some help. Maybe the nanny girl would even drive them back to the hotel. That is, if she was at the party. Ira suspected that she would be. No, he *knew* that she would be. She hadn't mentioned a party, but he knew that she would be there. Perhaps that had been her secret.

He strode ahead, moving away from Myra, anxious to get to the party and find company. He wasn't that bothered about getting back to the hotel anymore. He suddenly just wanted to get to the party. Some need drove him on, mixed with the fear that the sounds would suddenly stop and he would be left in the darkness with only Myra for company.

He vaguely heard Myra call from behind, but her voice was indistinct in the noise from the party that was getting nearer and nearer. He turned one last corner and saw it. The party. It was a street party, with trestle tables laid out down the centre of the road. It was a long, wide avenue, perhaps a mile long, but the party filled the whole road. The tables were covered in red and white checked cloth and bulged with all manner of party food; it reminded Ira of the summer fetes back in Kansas when he had been a boy. There were people thronging the street and Ira hung back, suddenly shy. He didn't know these people; how could he expect them to invite him to their party? He felt dirty, ashamed for presuming too much. He started to turn away when a voice pulled him back. It was her, the girl from before; she was at the party as he had known she would be. The little girl, whose head he had patted, was wrapped around her legs. Both were smiling at him. She spoke.

"You found us. I'm so glad. I knew that you would, that you understood. Please join us."

She took his arm and led him into the throng.

Myra turned the corner of the street only moments after Ira had disappeared round it. She fully expected to see his little fat figure shuffling down the street towards this so-called party that only he could hear. She was getting sick of him and filled her lungs, ready for yelling. When she turned the corner her breath was expelled without sound. In front of her was a wide avenue, perhaps a mile in length. The streetlights illuminated the whole road almost as if it was daylight. She gasped. Ira had gone.

9.10 a.m.

The dead guy beside me on the bed grunts and turns over as I wake and sit up. He wasn't there when I crashed out last night, but nothing surprises me these days. Not since the world went nuts. I poke him in the ribs, grimacing slightly as my finger enters the side of his torso, round about the level where his kidneys are. He doesn't react. I gaze at the gloop on my finger then speak.

"Hey, man. Get off my bed."

He ignores me so I get off the bed instead and go downstairs. In the lounge a vampire is sitting in the chair watching old horror films and laughing. She ignores me too; it's my house but they don't seem to care. None of them.

There's a creature in the kitchen eating the breakfast cereal that I scrounged from the looted supermarket, but I'm not going to argue with something that I don't recognize. Especially when it has fangs a foot long. Instead I go out into the fresh new day, under the new pink coloured sky.

9.20 a.m.

The dark pall over central London shows me where They came through. I haven't gone over in that direction yet, towards Westminster and the river, and I don't want to. Hampstead is close enough. John told me that he actually saw Them come through a rip beside the Thames, but I'm not convinced that he actually saw it. He does have a tendency to exaggerate.

The dead guy hanging from the lamppost smiles at me and waggles his fingers, the same way he does every morning. Today I manage to smile back. After all, the guy's only doing his job. I still don't know why he got strung up, or who did it. Maybe I should ask him.

The street is empty of traffic, as it has been for the last few months. I don't know what happened to the rest of the people; I woke one morning to find all this. There are a few people still around, but only very few.

Well, there are only a few normal people still around. I mean, people who are actually still alive. Dead people you can find by the bucket load.

I don't know what happened, but it must have been like Judgement Day, with the dead all coming back. Unfortunately, it seemed like a lot of other things came back with them.

It's not like it is terribly dangerous or anything. The dead are either non-committal towards the few who are still living or they try to be friendly. It's Them you've got to be careful of. Those nasty buggers that came through the rip. Still, if you don't bother Them, they tend not to bother you.

10 a.m.

I find myself in a deserted deli near to Hampstead tube station. I don't like to go too close to the tube stations. Too many weird noises from down below. I'm picking through the tinned stuff next to a naked woman with maggots in her hair and a demon who is sniffing over the champagne when howls and screams echo in from the street outside. The woman turns to look and her head falls off. I stifle a giggle. I still have my manners. The demon picks up a bottle of '91 Bollinger and plucks out the cork with one claw. It takes a swig and wipes its mouth. It looks at me and speaks.

"Nice."

The screams from outside continue, but I'm more surprised at the fact that the demon has spoken to me. After all, we haven't been introduced.

"I'm sure it is."

He offers me the bottle. I think vaguely about demon germs then decide that it couldn't make much difference. I take a good long swig. It is nice champagne. I give the bottle back and speak.

"Charles. Charles Wheeler."

I stick my hand out. He shakes it with a claw that feels like a dry leather glove. My hand comes back to me bleeding.

"CZZXHRE"

"Pardon?"

"Chris."   A smile accompanies the translation.

"What's happening outside?"

"Idiot. Shoot at us. We kill for fun."

"Oh."

"Don't worry. Safe. You."

"Good. Thank you."

He waves a goodbye and disappears out of the broken front window to join his unseen companions. Not a bad chap.

10.30 a.m.

I wander across the heath as I eat my breakfast. The place is empty. Both the dead and Them seem to prefer the city streets and not open spaces. Weird.

I can see things moving at the edge of the heath but can't make out what they are from this distance. Could be anything. I mean that, they literally could be anything. The weirdest looking things came out of that rip.   All the way from things that were inside-out to perfectly normal looking reptilian demons.

The birds are still singing happily in the trees around me.   The noise cheers me up.   I used to think about suicide but I guessed fairly quickly that there would be no peace in death.

Noon

The bottled beer is warm, but not too bad. A dead couple sit kissing in one of the booths of the pub while something green chews on the man's foot.   I take another swig. It's tempting to drown one's sorrows, but that's the easy way out. Drugs are okay and there are plenty of them, but I don't indulge that often.   It pays to keep one's senses round here. The green thing runs off clutching a toe, but the man doesn't notice.

I finish my beer and start on the warm G&T, which is my main course for lunch.   I lied about not drowning ones sorrows; the day goes faster when you've got a buzz on. Out of the corner of my eye I see that the guy is trying to mount the girl. Dear god, have they no restraint? Mind, it's not often you get a live…sorry, a dead sex show during lunch. I start on liquid dessert.

1 p.m.

I find myself on the edge of Camden and decide to walk down to the lock. I walk past the place where the market used to be and reach the lock. Something with tentacles is scrabbling around on the quayside but most of the creature is still in the canal. I walk quickly past it but I'm no danger; it seems more interested in the rubbish bins that it is trying to get hold of.

Life is weird, but it's normal at the same time. Here I am in the middle of a holiday camp for Hell, but life for me is drab and boring. No clubs, no pubs, no friends, no more West End shopping. No more West End. What a mess. Suicide flits through my mind again but I still can't think of way to do it so that I wouldn't come back. Dynamite? I have a vision of me as a cartoon character, getting blown into tiny bits. Maybe it would work, but where the hell do you get dynamite? And what would I look like if the bits did come back together again?

Something that looks like a troll or an orc or something shambles past me going in the opposite direction, but it ignores me. It's clutching a half-chewed leg in its paw.

I get past the canal and notice movement on a bit of grass near to the road. I decide to check it out. There are about three or four bodies moving around on the grass and it takes me a good minute or two to work out that they are alive and that they are fighting. It takes me a moment longer to realise that it isn't a fight; it's a rape. Three men on one woman. I can't decide what to do, so I puke on my shoes and then start running. First away, then towards them. In all these weeks I haven't seen the demonic inhabitants of London do anything as barbaric.

The first man is standing with his back to me. I push him and run past him. I don't wait to see what he's going to do and head instead towards the other two, who by now have noticed my presence. One is mounting the woman, who I still can't see properly, and the other is holding her. Both watch my arrival without reaction. I stop. The one holding the woman reaches inside his jacket and pulls out a silver automatic pistol, like the ones they used to have on the television. I feel the bullet hit my stomach and then all feeling goes out of my body and I fall to the ground.

10 p.m.

I get back to my house by about 10pm. The vampire is still watching videos, but now she's sniggering over comedy films.

The dead guy is still on my bed. He's reading a book upside-down. I realise with an imagined thump in my still chest that eventually I will be the same as him, forgetful and vacant. He looks up and smiles at me, we are kindred spirits now. Perhaps I will go down to Westminster tomorrow and investigate the rip. It's not as if I'm in any danger anymore.

"What a noise! What is that man doing down there? I tell you Deirdre, that man downstairs is always making some sort of noise. He has visitors at all times of the day and night. It's unbearable. I might have to phone the landlord again."

"Yes, Agatha," replied her listless companion, who hadn't really been listening to Agatha's complaints. There was noise from the flat below, but it wasn't that bad, mainly footsteps and talking, but Agatha was very fussy. It wouldn't have bothered Deirdre.

Agatha had been in the bedsit for about six months, since the death of her husband Derek. He had been a self-employed businessman. It wasn't until after his demise, when his accountant and the taxman finally got round to assessing his worth, that it had been discovered that he had died heavily in debt. Agatha had lost the house, the Jag and the respect of her friends in Acacia Avenue. Deirdre was the only one who still kept in touch, but that was more from an elevated sense of sympathy that any real feeling of friendship.

"Well, it is terrible. I've complained to the landlord, but he doesn't care. Such a horrible little man. When I think of my Derek, it breaks my heart."

Her voice trailed off into dry sobs. Deirdre didn't try to console her, her sympathy only stretched so far and in her opinion it was time that Agatha started to look to the future. Agatha continued to sniff, more for effect than from real emotion. Deirdre stood up.

"Well, Agatha, I must be going now. George will be home soon."

Agatha stood as well and dried the rest of her tears. No-one understood how she felt.

"Will you come round next week?"

"I'll have to see, it depends on the ladies at the golf club. They've arranged a coffee morning."

Agatha, who had been forced out of the golf club when she couldn't pay her fees, sniffed in disapproval.

"Well, come round if you are free."

Deirdre left, after giving her friend a cursory peck on the cheek. Agatha went to the window to watch her friend walk to her car parked on the rather scruffy street. Deirdre had to push past a variety of obstacles including three dust-bins, rubbish spilling from them, and two drunks who were sprawled on the steps of the building. Agatha turned away and looked round the two rooms that she now occupied. In her most cheerful moments she had to admit that it was a dingy little hole. When she was 'down', as she put it, she called it far worse but it was all she could afford now that she was forced to live on welfare benefits. Derek's death had left her with nothing, in fact it had left her with less than nothing. She still owed large amounts of money to the bank.

Her bedsit was situated in a large Victorian house, which at one time had been elegant and beautiful. It had obviously been built for the gentry. Agatha remembered from her childhood the family that had used to live in the house. They had obviously been such nice people, even if Agatha's family hadn't been of sufficient class to be able to socialize with them. It was a shame that the building had been sold to an absentee landlord who only visited the place to do one of three things; show people round, throw people out or collect the rent. The welfare paid Agatha's rent directly to him, so she had very little to do with him except to complain bitterly and frequently about the man downstairs.

The man downstairs had moved in about two months after she had arrived. She had seen him from her window as he arrived, although she had thought nothing of it at the time. He was a small man, with a thin pointy face. Agatha hadn't liked the look of him at all and when she found out that he had taken the flat below her, she resolved to try to avoid him as much as possible. That in itself hadn't been a difficult thing to achieve. She had a clear view of all the comings and goings from her window and when she saw him leave she knew that she was clear to do the same.

It was the noise from below that drove her mad. It wasn't as if the man downstairs had parties all night, or played loud music. In fact, in many ways he was a very good neighbour. It was just the constant footsteps and conversation that continually intruded on her peace of mind. Agatha sometimes stood for hours at her window watching a variety of visitors coming and going from the flat below. People of all types, from common people to quite respectable looking types visited the man downstairs. A person of a more suspicious nature would have suspected that the man downstairs was dealing in drugs, but Agatha, who had been brought up to be a lady, hadn't even considered that as an option.

It annoyed her. The constant to-ing and fro-ing irritated her because there was never any peace from it. The man downstairs rarely left his flat and when he was home there was a constant stream of visitors.

She turned back to the window and saw that Deirdre was safely gone. On one nightmarish occasion, just after she had moved in and when the other ladies from Acacia Avenue were still speaking to her, one of the drunks had shown Barbara Jenkins his penis. Presumably it had shocked her because Mr. Jenkins wasn't in the habit of doing that sort of thing to his wife. Maybe, Agatha had thought, rather nastily, that Barbara had been reminded of something that she hadn't had in a long time. Either way, it had been the end of Barbara Jenkin's visits. Only Deirdre still visited her, but Agatha knew that her visits were begrudged.

Agatha saw another stranger arriving at the front door and presently she heard the door of the flat downstairs being opened. The voices started up. Five minutes passed and then the door below was opened again and Agatha, who had stayed in place during the visit, saw the stranger leave. He looked happy. What was going on down there?

She decided, with sudden middle-class self-righteous clarity, to find out what was going on downstairs. If she could present evidence to the landlord regarding the cause of all that noise, then he would be forced to do something about the man downstairs. Hopefully, it would lead to a quick eviction. She was pleased. Finally, after all these months of grieving, in one split second, her true spiteful, intrusive Acacia Avenue nature was back. She stood at her window, waiting for the next person to visit the man downstairs. She didn't have to wait long.

She waited until the visitor, a man of about forty, had entered the flat and then listened for the voices to start. When they did she walked across to her front door, opened it and crept out onto the landing. Below, she could just make out the door of the flat below. It was closed. Good.

She started down the stairs, careful not to stand on any of the squeaky boards. She didn't want to attract any attention to herself. Luckily the hallway was empty and, apart from the drunks on the doorstep, the whole house might as well have been deserted. She reached the ground floor and moved across to the doorway belonging to the flat of the man downstairs. Voices could be heard through the thin wood. Agatha stood close enough to hear what was being said, whilst pretending to read the faded and scruffy list of house rules that were pinned up nearby. She could hear the conversation from within quite clearly.

"So, you know why you've come here?"

That had to be the man downstairs.

"Yes."

That had to be his visitor.

"Then, since you are here of your own free will, I must ask the question that you are here to answer. Once you answer and I have agreed, the deal will have been done. There is no need for paper, our contract will be verbal. Understand?"

"Yes."

The voice of the man downstairs changed to an eerie whisper. Agatha could feel the hairs on the back of her neck rise.

"What do you want from me?"

"Wealth and power."

There was a pause.

"Granted. The deal is made."

Agatha guessed that the conversation, and therefore the visit, was over. She just managed to move across to the other side of the hallway before the visitor left the flat. She pretended to be walking towards the stairs, but the man ignored her anyway. His face was flushed and he looked neither looked right nor left as he made a quick exit from the house. Agatha was none the wiser about what was going on in the flat downstairs, but she was now definite that something untoward was occurring. Something made her look up and she glanced towards the flat belonging to the man downstairs. She realised with a start that he was standing in the doorway looking at her. He spoke.

"You really shouldn't listen at other people's doors, Agatha."

She spluttered, but said nothing. Something told her there was no point lying.

"Come in."

It wasn't a request. The inside of the flat downstairs looked very much like her own. It lacked the tasteful trinkets that she had salvaged from Acacia Avenue but, apart from that, it was very similar. The man stood in the centre of the lounge and smiled.

"You've been very interested in my affairs."

It was another statement.

"Well, yes."

She felt that she might as well agree to something that he already knew.

"I don't mind. I'm used to all this attention. Just tell me one thing. What do you want from me?"

She didn't realise the implications of her answer, instead favouring a standard middle-class reply.

"I want some peace and quiet."

He smiled and at last she saw the darkness in his eyes. He spoke.

"Granted. The deal is made."

Then, much to her amazement and with a dawning realization of what she had just agreed to, the man from downstairs disappeared.

Checking his watch for the umpteenth time that day, he nodded in satisfaction. It was five o'clock and he was ready. Ready for their first Christmas together as husband and wife. Glancing round the lounge, he checked one last time to ensure that everything was in place and just right. She would be home from work soon and he wanted it all to be perfect for her. It was a shame that she had to work on Christmas Eve, but he had just lost his job and that meant that she had to work as many hours as possible to keep up with the bills. He felt bad about it, but he did his best to make sure the house was tidy and that there was always a meal ready for her when she got home.

He was satisfied. The room looked like a scene from a Christmas movie. The logs in the fireplace were burning brightly and the mantelpiece was festooned with a festive garland of holly, ivy and spruce. Pinned to the mantelpiece were their Christmas stockings; two green and blue oversized socks, complete with embroidered names. They were a surprise for her, she didn't know that he had ordered them. He had decided to hang them early, in an attempt to make her laugh when she got home. He hoped that she would find it funny and it just might become one of their personal Christmas traditions.

The Christmas tree sat in the corner of the lounge, resplendent with twinkling lights and sparkling baubles. They had gone out the previous weekend to a local tree farm to select the perfect tree. It was a little bit too big for the room, but it was the perfect shape. You couldn't beat having a real tree.

He had placed various Christmas decorations round the room. A pair of small pottery Victorian street scenes, backlit with tea-lights, sat on the mantelpiece. On the dresser was a small porcelain Christmas tree, complete with a tiny train winding its way up towards the star that crowned the top. Candles, dotted around the room added to the ambience.

From the kitchen came the delicious smells of wine being mulled, ham being baked and chestnuts being roasted. He was planning a very traditional Christmas Eve meal for them. The turkey, the star of the show, was waiting in the refrigerator, ready for the big day tomorrow.

He glanced at his watch again, if her train had been on schedule then she would be at the station by now, climbing into her car to make the short drive home. He knew the roads were clear of snow, so it shouldn't take her too long.

Glancing once more round the room, he realised that the fire could do with more wood. There was no more wood indoors, he would have to get some logs from outside. Stepping out of the front door, he paused to reflect just how perfect the scene was. Their house was rural, with only one close neighbour. From the front porch he could see sweeping vistas of fields and trees. Winter had only just arrived in the region. It had been green until just a few days ago, then the snow had arrived blanketing the area in a thick coat. The fir trees in the garden now looked like the snow covered trees depicted in the Christmas cards on their mantelpiece. The driveway had been ploughed, but apart from that, the snow was pristine and untouched. Moonlight bathed the front garden in a cold light. It was so beautiful. He decided that he would suggest to her that after their meal they wrap up warm and go outside to admire the view.

He walked to the wood pile that lay about thirty feet from the house. The firewood had been stacked under the overhanging branches of an evergreen tree, to protect it from the worst of the snow. Despite that precaution the logs at the top were lightly dusted. He glanced back at the house, their home. It was a nineteenth century farmhouse, red-brick with a wooden veranda on three sides. It was a solid, welcoming house, especially now, with the amber light shining through the front windows, contrasting against the whiteness of the world outside.

Suddenly he froze. The firewood that he held in his arms fell to the ground. The vision in front of him had changed. Instead of that welcoming home at Christmastime, he saw a terrifying vision. It was the same house he was looking at, but it was no longer his home. This version of the house was dark and cold, and in the moonlight he could see that the roof was gone and the windows were dark and broken. It was the burnt-out shell of the home that he knew and loved. As he stared at that dreadful sight, something horribly familiar stirred in his memory. A vision unbidden and unwanted flashed through his mind.

In the vision he was back in the house. He dumped the fire wood in the basket next to the fireplace. Doing some last minute rearranging before she came home, he knocked over a candle on the fireplace; it hit the stockings, causing an instant conflagration. Suddenly there was fire and smoke. He was screaming. He clutched his throat, he couldn't breathe. His arms flailed about in front of him. He couldn't see, couldn't find his way out. He could feel the heat on his face, vaguely aware of the flames as they exploded from the fireplace and flowed like liquid over the Christmas tree. He felt himself stumble over furniture as he tried to escape. The noise of cracking wood and collapsing timbers was insanely loud.

The whole house was in flames. He fell to his knees in the smoke, blinded and choking.

Cool air brought him back to his senses. The terrifying sensations subsided and he found that his vision had cleared and his breathing had eased. He was still outside, kneeling in the cold snow next to the woodpile.

He glanced up at the house, expecting the worst, but it was back to normal. The idyllic Christmas home was back, with no sign of the derelict wreck that had terrified him just a few moments ago. He shook his head, but the memory of the burning, choking sensations remained. It had all been too real, as if it had really happened. Forgetting the extra firewood, he suddenly knew that he had to get back to the house. If he didn't, all would be lost. He would be lost. He started to run, stumbling in the knee-deep snow. He didn't look where he was running, his eyes were fixed firmly on the house, praying it would stay as the warm, welcoming home he loved. He knew, absolutely knew, that if he didn't make it back to the house then he would never see her again. The house would remain as the burnt out shell and they would never have their first Christmas together. He had to make it.

Stumbling onto the veranda, feeling more exhausted than he ever had done before, he pushed open the front door. Was it too late? Was everything lost? Warm amber light welcomed him. He felt tears in his eyes. He had made it in time. He walked into the lounge, ready to welcome her when she finally came home.

I

The first sensation he felt was the warm sunshine on his face. It warmed his aching, tired muscles and made him smile. He found himself walking down a crowded street. All around him milled groups of shoppers, enjoying the warm weather and the bright yellow sunlight. But he heard no noise, no buzz of conversation. He was only aware of the warm sunshine and the happy faces as he strolled down the summer streets. He felt no emotion, except a deep feeling of sublime ease, of peace with this world.

The street ended, and he found himself walking on a wide boulevard, bordered on one side by a park and on the other by tall, imposing buildings formed from a light coloured stone. Vivid green trees and shrubs burst forth from the park in stark contrast to the monochromatic shading of the buildings. In this wider avenue he could only focus on that which was directly in front of him. To his left and right he could only make out indistinct figures and shapes.

A voice spoke to him, the first sound that he had heard. He froze. The voice spoke again.

"...blocked by an overturned car just past junction twenty-one. All southbound lanes are closed for at least two hours. Now, to ease those traffic blues, the number two sound in the charts this week..."

He woke. He turned his head briefly into the pillow, trying to get back to sleep. The combined sound of the radio and the rain against the window conspired noisily to wake him again. He rose, dissatisfied. Half-remembered images from the dream flashed through his mind as he wobbled down to the toilet. He rubbed his bleary eyes, trying to clear his vision.

As he used the toilet he tried to focus on his dream, but the images faded as he slowly reached full consciousness. Walking back out into the kitchen he looked round his house. It was dark and cold. The furniture and the pictures looked dreary and lifeless compared to the bright sunlight of his dream world. He turned on the kettle and started to make himself breakfast. The rain, unchanged, continued to pour down from the heavens onto his world.   Suddenly he realised the time and made a scramble for work, knowing that it was already too late.

II

It was the same wide boulevard again. The sun, as always, was shining. He was aware of noise, a gentle burbling river of sound. It was the noise of people as they moved around the city. But he couldn't see their faces. They were indistinct blurs.

He walked endlessly along the highways of the city. One minute he was back on the wide boulevard, the next in a jumbled market with people rushing around him as he walked. Sometimes he found himself in quiet residential areas, with no other people around. There was no order to his progression. He wandered wherever he wanted to go.

Then, he saw her. Hers was the first face that he could properly focus on. She was blonde and pretty, dressed in light coloured clothes. Her bright white teeth flashed in the sunlight as she laughed with the others around her. He loved her as soon as he saw her. And he knew that she would love him back. Forever.

The doorbell rang suddenly, waking him violently from his dream. He wrenched himself out of bed and scrambled downstairs, answering some modern instinct triggered by the persistent bell. It was the milkman, standing in the rain.

"Three forty-one, mate."

He paid from the scattered change on the telephone table beside the door. The milkman turned on his heel and left without a thank you.

"Crap," he grumbled. He stood, a scruffy mess, in soiled pyjamas and a flea-bitten dressing gown. He remembered, and her face came back to him, as vivid as reality. More so. He smiled suddenly, knowing that this vision would not fade.

He wandered into the kitchen and glanced at the dusty clock. It was half past nine. He had slept through the alarm. Already an hour late for work, he called in sick, unable to face the reality of the factory after his dream. All he wanted to do was get back there. He went to the kitchen drawer and opened it. Lying nestled in-between a candle and some batteries was a small brown bottle. Sedatives. The ones she had been taking right up until her death. He squeezed the thought of that from his mind. Couldn't bear to think of it. Couldn't stand that reality. The pills were years old and he wondered if they would do the trick; would they take him back to that other, more acceptable reality? Taking three rather than the prescribed dose of one, he wandered back upstairs through the dusty, cold house.

III

He was with her at last. She was holding him close as they walked through the city. They were together. He felt confident and sure. They walked down the wide boulevard, laughing. She turned to hold him tight for a second then was gone, moving away from him. He chased after her.

They were suddenly at the coast, on a beach. As always, the sun was shining.

Then they were in the mountains, purple and green with heather. Deep pools of water lay between the peaks.

They travelled suddenly and without sensation to a beautiful, dappled glade bathed in green light. Then to a tiny village. They were everywhere together. He didn't mind where. They were together. That was all that counted.

He woke. It was mid-afternoon. Outside, the rain still poured down. He could sleep no more. The pills had worn off, their effectiveness diluted by time. He went downstairs, feeling queasy and bleary-eyed. The dream flowed through his mind. He barely noticed the house, the rooms unchanged since her demise. He saw nothing except her. He had to get back.

He opened the drawer and removed the bottle of pills. He shook it gently, listening to the rattle. At least twenty were left. He opened the lid and poured the contents onto the table, avoiding the dirty crockery and pans. He scooped up all the pills and put them in his mouth. He took a draught of water from the tap and swallowed painfully. He went back upstairs.

IV

They were in a park, sitting on a bench, enjoying the bright yellow sunlight. Above them was a small hill, the beginning of the mountain range through which they had wandered. In front of them, in the distance, he could see the sea and the coast. The water sparkled a deep blue. At the edge of the park there were light coloured buildings. He could see people moving around as they walked through the summer streets. Nothing was out of focus. Everything was real. At last. She turned to him and spoke for the first time.

"I've missed you."

He turned to her.

"I've missed you too."

She smiled and held him.

They found him five days later, when the milkman reported his absence. They broke down the door. He was lying in his bed, at peace at last. The milkman, who had followed the policeman upstairs, spoke.

"He was a right weirdo, him. Especially after his wife died, years back. Never had a girlfriend in all the years after she died. Never. That's not normal."

The policeman ignored the milkman and stared down at the body. The face of the corpse looked serene and happy, as if all cares and worries had been lifted from it. Even in the grey, dirty house with the rain pelting against the window it looked as if the man's face was bathed in sunlight. Bright yellow sunlight.

Desert. Nothing but empty, boundless desert, stretching for miles and miles. For years and years. It was endless the time that he had spent searching this desolation. The wasteland that had once been the mortals' proud and lofty civilisation. He had seen countless great ruins of cities and cathedrals. All tombs now, containing the dust of humanity. He had spent an eternity walking past them, through them, never ceasing and never returning. One lost, lonely figure in a deserted landscape.

He was the last of his kind, the last on Earth. Maybe even the very last sentient creature on the surface or in the seas of the dead planet. The disease that had taken all the plants and animals had not affected him or those that had been like him. The insignificant virus that had destroyed life more violently and more quickly than the biggest bomb had by-passed his kind. But in a way it had affected all his tribe. Did the lion not starve and die when the antelope became extinct? Did not even the great all-conquering virus fade to nothing once all life on Earth passed into the veil of night? His tribe had starved as the lion had but alas, unlike the great cat, they had been unable to die. Instead, theirs had been the torture of endless pain, of endless torment and hunger. All the others had finally chosen the Great Sleep rather the pain of the conscious existence. The Great Sleep, the dark dormancy where bodies decayed to dust as the spirit faded to nothing. Not death, but close. But he had been different; loving the thin shadow of life that he still clung to. It was too precious, and he was too selfish and too scared to give it up. And so he wandered the world, hoping that he would find the elixir that would resurrect and energise his weakened muscles.

He came to the sea, powerful and restless. Like his own spirit. Life would come again, he knew that. As a child of the planet, as a part of nature, he knew that somewhere in the darkest depths life was probably already stirring. But it would be centuries or more until he would find the liquid he needed. He could not wait. He almost envied his friends who had gone before him. To the darkness. At least their pain was over.

He headed back to the land. He knew he would find nothing in the water. He came to the ruins of another destroyed town and took shelter. The cold wind did not affect him, but he still found the sensation unpleasant. A wall shielded him from the worst of the sea breeze. His delicate nostrils picked up the scents of the ocean. He loved its smell. Suddenly his nostrils flared. There had been something briefly in the air. Something he had not smelt for decades, longer even. A human smell. The distinctive odour of human blood. His heart would have raced, if it had been capable of such an action. He stood, to try and pick up the scent again. There it was. It came from the land, not the sea. It was far away, but he could follow the trace. He had found what he had been looking for. What he had denied the Great Sleep for. Prey.

It took him three weeks to find the source of the bewitching smell. It was deep in the desert, far within the driest, hottest part. Constantly walking, day and night, he traversed miles and miles of sand dunes and scrubland. His body tissue dried and became desiccated as he travelled; his ancient skin crisped on his head and arms, peeling away to nothing. No new skin grew back; he had long ago lost that power, but he no longer cared about his appearance; there was no-one to see him.

He did not feel the sun sear his body with a strength that would have killed any mortal. He felt nothing at all. Only the thought of that wonderful odour filled his mind. Thoughts of the beautiful life-giving elixir drove him onwards.

He came across the isolated ruins at night. He found the remains of a wall to rest against. His muscles were fatigued. He had driven himself hard, maybe too much, but it didn't matter. The only thing that mattered was the prey. And now he was at the source. The odour was strongest here, somewhere within these destroyed dwellings. He closed his eyes. Morning would be soon enough to search. For the first time in centuries he was tired. Not physically, no, that was impossible. No, he was mentally drained. He felt old.

The dawn warmed his eyelids, forcing him to open his eyes. He welcomed the light, he could now search with his eyes as well as his nose. It didn't take him long to locate his prey. A brief search through the ruins yielded nothing. It had been a small town, probably no more than a village. It was a dead place now. The source was just outside the town; a metal lid embedded in the sand. A manhole cover with a lever mechanism attached. The entrance to a bunker. He knelt in the sand and put his face to the metal between lid and base. A slight draught from below blew the powerful smell of human into his nostrils. His sensations were overloaded by the odour. At last. The smell of fresh prey.

The cover bore silver streaks in the otherwise dulled and weatherworn metal. It was obvious that it had been recently opened. And closed again. It was now just a matter of waiting. He found a spot on a dune about a hundred yards from the entrance and settled down to wait.

It was nearing the end of the day when there were signs of life from the entrance. A quiet, rusty creak woke him from his doze. The lid was being pushed sideways to open it. He saw a patch of light coloured hair move above the metal lip, but nothing else. The rest of the head eventually poked out. It moved from side to side, obviously checking out the terrain. Despite overwhelming excitement, he remained motionless, knowing that with the sinking sun behind him he would be difficult to spot. After a moment the figure emerged completely from the hole in the sand. It headed towards the ruins, clutching a bucket under one arm. It passed close to him without noticing and, taking the advantage, he leapt out at the figure. It squeaked and fell in the sand, the bucket's contents spilling. The figure, spread-eagled, used an arm to shield itself.

"Don't hurt me! Please!"

It was the first time in decades that he had heard human speech. He stood frozen, entranced by the sound. He had forgotten how beautiful a human voice could be. The figure lowered its arm slightly, obviously confused that there had been no attack, and in doing so exposed its face. He stared in surprise. The figure in front of him was a child, no more than ten years old. The child started to weep. He opened his mouth to speak to the child in front of him, all thoughts of attack and killing gone from his mind. His throat was too dry. He swallowed and tried again.

"Don't cry. I'm not going to hurt you. Please stop."

The figure stopped crying, snuffled and stared up at him in silence. He thought of something else to say.

"What's your name?"

The figure looked suspiciously at him, then spoke.

"Adam. What's yours?"

"Well, Adam, my name is…"

He suddenly realised he couldn't remember his own name. He stared down at his hands. His ancient hands. He couldn't remember his own name. Adam sat up, no longer scared.

"What is it then?"

"I don't know Adam. I've forgotten"

"My mummy wrote my name down for me. On a tag round my neck," Adam said helpfully. "That's how I remember. Didn't your mummy write your name down?"

"No, I don't remember her," he replied, but that knowledge was neither shocking nor new. A thought came to him.

"Is your mummy down in the bunker?"

Adam shook his head once, side to side.

"No, she is gone, like the rest."

"Gone? Do you mean dead?"

"Yes, she died about a month ago. I looked after them all, but they all died. They were ill. I've been by myself for ages and now the toilet has blocked up and I can't fix it."

Adam started to cry again.

"Then there is no-one else down there?"

"No. I'm lonely. Are you lonely?"

He stared at Adam, thoughts of prey coming back to him. Here in front of him was the first living human he had seen in decades. The first hint of fresh blood in all that time. Adam was probably the last human alive on the planet, certainly the only one he had come across in all his wanderings. The bunker must have been a survival shelter where Adam's forefathers had retreated to when the crisis had started. Adam's tribe would have been too scared to come out of their fortress, preferring to live underground on what they could grow under the earth. But then, some infection had ripped through the isolated group, sparing only the youngest and most helpless. How ironic.

The blood in Adam's veins would taste sweet and rich, but he couldn't do it. He couldn't bring himself to kill the precious life in front of him. Maybe the thing he craved most now was not blood, but company. Someone to share the empty world with.

Maybe through Adam he could eventually remember his own name. He replied.

"Yes, I am lonely. Do you want to come with me, Adam? We can go exploring. Maybe find some other people."

Adam nodded.

"Come on then, Adam. Let's go."

Ian stood on the platform, waiting for the last train home. He was dressed in what he considered to be standard business attire. Brown shoes, charcoal suit and a black overcoat. His tie was a shade of burgundy and his shirt was white. He worked downtown in the main headquarters of a national bank. He worked on the computer systems that supported the international banking division. He didn't mind his job.

The train drew into the station and slid slowly along the platform. Ian was bumped and jostled by the commuters waiting on the platform for the same train. He didn't mind, it was the same every night.

His home was about an hour north of the city. They had chosen to live in a moderate sized house further away from the city, instead of in a tiny apartment closer to the city. He didn't mind the commute.

He sat on the train in his usual spot, gazing out the window as the train passed through endless industrial estates and sub-divisions. It was November and already dark, but the street-lights allowed him to see the view as the train passed by. It was a view that he was used to. He had been riding this same line for nearly five years.

As he gazed into the twilight he could see his face reflected in the window. It wasn't a handsome face, very ordinary really. He had got used to his face a long time ago. He didn't really care, his wife Lucy loved him for who he was.

He had a solid, secure job, a lovely wife and a nice house. In a funny sort of way, that made his decision to kill himself all the more puzzling. Well, perhaps only to those who would try to figure out why he had done it. He knew why. He knew how dark he felt about his life. Yes, to an outsider it was clear that he had everything that he had ever wanted and there was no doubt his life, although perfectly ordinary to some, was enviable to many. But for many years he had felt an overwhelming despair. A dark depression about the pointlessness of life. He had seen many amazing things, but even the sight of the Grand Canyon or the falls at Niagara couldn't lift the overwhelming darkness in his soul. For many years now he knew that suicide was the only option for him. To find the peace denied to him in life. He hadn't ever sought help, knowing that he didn't want it; that no amount of counselling could help him avoid this ultimate destiny. All humans died, he had just decided to take on the responsibility himself. He knew that Lucy and his family would be devastated. Blame themselves. He had tried to express himself properly in his suicide note, try to explain himself. He hoped that it would be enough. They would find it in his briefcase, near to the spot on the bridge where he intended to jump into the river that flowed into the lake. The drop was a good hundred feet, but if that didn't do the job, then the water temperature at this time of year would finish him off. He had briefly considered using the very train that he was riding on as the instrument of his demise. So many others had. But he decided against it for two reasons. Firstly, his death would inconvenience hundreds of commuters and he didn't want anyone thinking badly of him. Secondly, it looked too damn painful. Simple as that.

The spot he had chosen was at the end of the line; a town called Lakeshore. It was situated, unsurprisingly, next to the lake, which was about forty miles north of his home. Instead of getting off at his normal station, he would continue on the train for another forty-five minutes, travelling as far north as was possible before the land gave way to the water. He could see his route in his mind, he had scouted it out a couple of times. He would step off the train, no doubt one of very few people getting off the train at that time of night. He would leave the station and walk about a mile towards the lakeshore. The road bridge crossed one of the main rivers entering the lake about a quarter of mile away from the lakeshore. He would walk along the pedestrian walkway at the side of the bridge. Reaching about halfway across, he would carefully place his briefcase against the guard rail, then he would climb the barrier. Then. He paused in his thoughts, he didn't need to think about that part of his plan. Not yet.

Despite the gravity of the journey, he felt himself dropping off to sleep. He decided not to fight it. Eyelids drooping, he glanced round the compartment. He saw that at this point in the journey there were only a few people accompanying him. The train had been travelling for about forty-five minutes and had passed most of the main commuter stations on the outskirts of the city. There were no more than a dozen people still remaining in the compartment. Most were sleeping. He dozed.

He woke with a jolt. It was pitch black outside and he had no idea where he was. His watch told him that he had already passed his normal stop. He had already passed the point of no return. He glanced around the compartment. It was empty. No surprise really, most of the people heading this far north would have got an earlier train. He looked out of the window, but the darkness was impenetrable. There was nothing outside. No lights. Nothing.

The train began to slow. Usually there was an announcement of the next station, but this time there was no cheerful conductor making wisecracks while making people aware of where they were. Ian suspected that these cheerful announcements were partially for customers new to the line, but mainly to wake those commuters who were in danger of sleeping through their stop.

Suddenly there was a flash of red outside the train. Ian strained to look backwards to see what it had been. A fire? An accident? The darkness obscured his view.

The train continued to slow. For some reason it was taking an inordinate amount of time to stop at the next station. The noise of the train changed from a distant rumble to a more immediate noise, almost as if the sound of the engine and wheels were echoing off tunnel walls. But there were no tunnels or underground sections this far north. He was sure of that. Yet, as he looked out of the window, he saw grimy, damp walls flashing by, illuminated by the light from the compartment.

The train finally stopped. Ian looked in amazement. He was in a subway station. A normal city subway station, complete with long platforms, a ticket booth and numerous turnstiles. He blinked slightly. Had he headed south without realising? No, it wasn't possible, the train wouldn't just head back south. Plus, the train was a massive, double decker commuter train, designed to move hundreds of people out of and into the city. It wasn't a subway train, it couldn't fit into the narrow tunnels. He looked for a station name. He saw an old-fashioned, enamelled sign on the wall. It read "*Styx*". Ian had never heard of that particular station, not on any of the routes. Must be a new one. But underground? This far north amongst the farmland, villages and lakes?

The platform was entirely deserted. The doors of the train wheezed open. Ian suddenly felt very alone and a little bit vulnerable. After a few moments, at the end of the compartment, a door opened and a tall figure appeared. He was dressed in the livery of an old fashioned conductor. There was no comfortable, fluorescent material on this individual. He was dressed in a black suit, with shiny brass buttons and a watch on a long chain. He wore a small peaked hat. For some reason Ian felt reassured. This guy was no doubt an old school type who had opted to wear the old-fashioned garb of a conductor, rather than the bright flashy uniform of the modern customer care representative. Ian liked it.

The figure passed him by without seemingly noticing him. Ian spoke.

"Excuse me, what station is this?"

The figure glanced round.

"This is Styx, Mr. Stevenson, as the sign outside states."

"You know my name?"

"Of course."

Ian didn't know how to respond to this. The conductor continued, as if he had been asked a question.

"I am Charon. I am the conductor. We will be joined by a great number of passengers momentarily."

Ian didn't know how to respond to this statement either, so he stayed quiet. The conductor touched the peak of his hat and moved on down the compartment. As he walked he started to call.

"All aboard! All aboard!"

He rang a small bell as he walked. Ian glanced outside onto the platform. Figures were now moving through the turnstiles and onto the train. Hundreds of them, patiently queuing to get through the turnstiles and then patiently waiting their turn to get onto the train. Normally a subway station would be a bustling, noisy place with people chatting and jostling to get on and off the trains. This vision was terrifyingly silent.

Ian watched as some of the figures entered his compartment. He saw that they were almost entirely grey. They shuffled along, with heads bowed. They were almost shadowy. He could have sworn on a couple of occasions he could see the furnishings of the compartment behind the figures, almost as if they were semi-transparent. He realised that his arm and neck hairs were standing on end, even though these sad, melancholy figures paid him no attention.

Ian was sitting in a four seat arrangement, with one seat next to him and two facing him. It was the standard seat layout on these trains. He felt a figure sit beside him, but dared not look. He couldn't help but look when the seat directly opposite him was occupied. He made eye contact. The figure in front of him was a young man. He looked bewildered and somehow despairing. Ian realised with a thump in his chest that he really could see the seat behind the figure. He was almost transparent, but his eyes were alive and conscious. Conscious and full of despair and desperation. If the eyes were the window to the soul, then this soul in front of him was suffering eternal torment.

"Hi," said Ian, in a lame attempt to find out what on earth was going on. There was no reply. Ian felt as if he had moved away from the life that he knew to some surreal dimension where things were not normal. Not real. He needed some answers. He said hello again, but the figure did not reply, it just stared at him. Suddenly the doors of the train closed and it started to move. Ian twitched. Where was this train heading to? Where were these figures, these people going? What was their final destination? Ian no longer thought that he was going to the lakeshore. His mind was no longer focused on his own plans. Now, he just wanted to get off this train.

The train picked up speed. In order to avoid looking at the ghastly spectre in front of him, Ian focused firmly on the outside view. The train was still in the tunnel, but as it moved forward Ian saw the tunnel end and the train emerge into what he presumed was the open air. He hoped vainly to see countryside and perhaps the occasional house or town, but the darkness was complete, nothing could be seen. Occasional flashes of red appeared, as they had done before, but Ian no longer thought that they were fires. He didn't want to think about what they could be. The door at the end of the compartment opened and the conductor reappeared.

"Tickets please. Get your tickets ready for inspection."

Charon moved down the corridor checking the ticket of each passenger. This normal everyday activity somehow reassured Ian. If this train company were interested in making sure everyone had a valid ticket, then this new world where he found himself couldn't be too strange.

The conductor arrived at the four seats where Ian was sat. The conductor looked directly at him.

"Ticket please, Mr. Stevenson."

Ian showed him the monthly pass that he used to travel on his daily commute. The conductor shook his head.

"This is not a valid ticket on this line. Not on this journey, not at this time. I must ask you to leave the train. Please come with me, sir."

Despite himself, Ian found himself rising and following the conductor. His fellow passengers ignored him, oblivious to one of their fellow passengers being removed. The conductor walked to the nearest door.

"You are not eligible to travel on this train, Mr. Stevenson. You do not have the required fare. You must leave."

The conductor pushed a button next to the door and with a growing horror Ian saw the door open. Outside he could see nothing, but the noise and rushing air told him that the train was going at some unimaginable speed. Was it credible that Charon was intending to push him off this train? He would be killed!

"Go," said the conductor.

He put his hand on Ian's shoulder and gently pushed. Ian had a blurred sensation of moving helplessly towards the door, into the darkness, and then there was nothing.

The hand shaking his shoulder woke him. The first thing he noticed was the blinding sunlight shining through the window of the train compartment. The second thing he noticed was that he was back in his seat, rather than standing in the doorway of the train. The third thing he noticed was that it wasn't Charon holding his shoulder but one of the usual customer care representatives that looked after the trains on this line.

"Hey buddy. Wake up!"

"Where I am?"

"Lakeshore. End of the line. You must have been on the last train up here last night. This is the first train of the day, about to head south to the city. I tell you, buddy, those late night crews are sloppy. Don't even check for guys like you before clocking off for the night. I should complain to the supervisor. Anyway buddy, I hope you don't mind me saying but you look like hell. You probably don't want to go to work looking like that."

Ian glanced down at himself. His suit was crumpled and stained with mud.

"No, I think I'll go for a walk then head home on the next train."

"Okay, buddy. See you later."

As Ian stepped off the train and stood on the platform, memories of previous night's train ride came flooding back. Where had he gone? Where were those people on the train going? He wasn't a stupid person. He knew that they were dead. That was the only explanation. Those people were on a journey to somewhere, perhaps somewhere not too pleasant. The memory of their eyes haunted him.

Ian straightened his tie and then reached into his briefcase. He removed the note, crumpled it and threw it into the nearest trash bin. Part of him thought he had experienced some sort of dream or hallucination, brought on by the subconscious stress of planning his own destruction. Part of him thought it might have been real. Perhaps it had been real. He didn't want to be a passenger on that train, boarding at Styx and journeying to an unknown destination under the care of Charon. Not yet, anyway. Not today. It was time to go and talk to his wife.

As he stared from the window of his office, he still found it difficult to see how he hadn't noticed it. It had lain there in the long grass for two months; all the way through the hottest summer in years, sweating and stinking and decaying in its own putrescence and all he had done was call the building supervisor and complain about the smell from the drains.

But it hadn't been the drains, had it? It had been that old man, lying dead no more than ten feet below his office window. His was the only occupied office on this side of the building and it should have been him that made the discovery.

The police weren't sure how the body got there, but they assumed that the man had wandered behind the office block looking for a place to relieve himself. The autopsy had indicated natural causes, a heart attack, and the evidence had proved that he had died where he was found. The inquest had given a verdict of accidental death. The alcohol level in the man's blood had been well above the expected average and that was considered to be a contributing factor in the death of an old man, ten feet below the window of an office belonging to him, Andrew Johnson.

The body had lain there for two months, eight whole weeks, before a dog allowed off the leash by its owner found the corpse and attracted enough attention to allow the subsequent discovery of the cadaver by its bemused and then disgusted owner.

That had been on a Saturday morning, when the building was empty, so none of them had known about it until the Monday morning when the police arrived to carry out interviews. He shivered at the memory.

They had taken him to the small room used for coffee breaks. Memories of him cracking jokes and chatting up the secretaries were now permanently tainted with the thought of the detectives' sharp, acid glances; they had been suspicious of him, he could see it in their eyes. How could a corpse lie un-noticed for eight whole weeks, right under his office window? The excuses of blocked drains and long grass hiding the body were obvious fabrications; he could see that thought in their minds. He could almost see the thought bubble appear from their heads; was this plump office worker sitting in front of them, a murderer? It was only with hindsight that he realised that the certainty of their suspicion was caused by his own guilt, making him feel responsible for another man's death.

The police knew the date the old man had gone missing, his wife had reported it, but they couldn't tell the exact time when he had died. They knew he had gone to the pub, but details on exactly what time he had left were sketchy. Was it possible that the man had actually staggered into those bushes under his window whilst he had been working at his desk? He had imagined the scenario a thousand times. The old guy, wobbling off the street, looking for a place to pee in private. He reaches for his fly, his bladder full to bursting, but instead clutches at his chest as the heart attack rips through his torso. He drops to his knees, seeing darkness descend, then falls forward onto his face as death comes for him. Flat on his face, where he was to lie for the next eight weeks.

Maybe he had cried out as he dropped, maybe he had been silent. Andrew would never have heard a cry anyway; the radio in his office was blaring constantly. Maybe if he'd switched it off, as he had been asked to by the boss on many occasions, then he would have heard the old man cry out and could have saved his life.

Andrew had read all about it in the local paper when the news had broken, on the Tuesday after the discovery. The old guy had been married, with five grown-up kids and an army of grandchildren and great-grandchildren. He had lived in a small terraced house in an area close to where Andrew lived. His family had reported him missing after he failed to come home and the local police had carried out some extensive searches, but who would have thought to look in the long grass behind an office block? The article had been the first time that Andrew had learnt the man's name. It had been Bernard Jones. He had been seventy-eight years old.

For no reason at all, Andrew went round to the old man's house about three weeks after the discovery of the body and stood outside, looking at the drawn curtains. There were a few cars outside, with people in dark clothes milling around. It was only after a few moments that the realization that he was watching the funeral clicked into place. A young man, noticing Andrew standing on the opposite side of the road, walked across.

"Can I help?"

Andrew started, unsure of what to say or do.

"Can I help?"

The man's expression, initially friendly and open, grew cold and unfriendly.

"No thank you. I'm just paying my respects to Bernard."

The man's expression immediately softened.

"Oh. I didn't realise that you knew my Grandfather. I thought you might have been the press again. They've been hanging around for weeks now. It was the way he was found, you see. Please, come into the house and say hello to Nan."

"No. Thank you. I must get back to work."

"Please. Grandad had so few friends. It would be so nice for her to see you. We're just back from the crematorium."

Against his will and better judgement, Andrew found himself being guided into the small house, where the entire Jones family was gathered for the funeral of their patriarch. It was a forlorn little house, showing too clearly that Bernard Jones had not been a rich man. The wallpaper in the hallway was too old and too thin to indicate anything else. Andrew was gently steered into the front room which bore an uncanny resemblance to his own grandparents' house. It was full of what his mum would have called knick-knacks. Plates with various pictures hung from the walls. Brass figures of dogs and horses stood on the mantelpiece above the gas fire. Photographs of the family were everywhere. Bernard might not have been rich in the financial sense, but he did have wealth of another kind. He was rich with family.

The room had two chairs and a sofa where an old woman sat. Andrew presumed that this was Mrs. Jones, widow. All around her sat and sprawled the real life equivalents of the photographs on the walls. Middle aged men and women, teenage girls and boys and children were arrayed around the matriarch of the Jones family. At least four generations were represented in the room. They all bore an uncanny resemblance to each other.

Snacks and drinks were spread round the room and Andrew had the impression that a lot of alcohol would be consumed in Bernard's name over the course of the afternoon.

Andrew stood there awkwardly, not knowing what to say. He shouldn't have been there, he didn't know the deceased or any of his family. He felt like a fool. He should have just stood up to the young man outside. The conversation stopped and interested faces turned towards him. Mrs. Jones smiled at him. The young man spoke.

"Nan, this is one of Grandpa's friends." He paused, "What's your name, mate?"

"Andrew. Andrew Johnson."

"Nice to meet you Mr. Johnson. Bernard never mentioned you, but that's no never mind."

A giggled whisper reached Andrew as he stood there, feeling sweat trickle down his back.

"Nice tie for a funeral."

He was wearing his cartoon tie, which he thought made him look like a fun guy. He didn't realise when he put it on this morning that he would be wearing it to a funeral. He blushed even more.

"Come and sit beside me Mr. Johnson and tell me how you knew Bernard. It's nice to hear stories about him. Makes me feel as if he's still with us. We were married for fifty-six years you know. Never had a row, not ever. We didn't have much money but we was happy."

Andrew sat, trying desperately to think his way out of the situation he had stumbled into.

"So, how did you know my Bernard?" asked Mrs. Jones once he was settled.

"Well…"

"It wasn't through the bingo was it? He loved the bingo, not that he ever won anything."

The others around her laughed.

"No, it wasn't through bingo."

"The pub then. He loved his ale."

A ragged cheer went up in the room and several of the men raised their plastic glasses to indicate the same preference.

"No, it wasn't the pub either."

A greasy plastic cup containing warm white wine was thrust into his hand. He took an involuntary sip just to avoid speaking for a moment.

"So where did you know him from then?"

There was no other answer than the truth and it spilled out of his mouth in an unchecked flow. As he spoke he watched the faces of the Jones family. They went from complacent enjoyment to amazement and then to anger. Mrs. Jones sat on the sofa beside him with an expression of stunned bemusement on her face. Tears welled out of her eyes and coursed down the canyons of her wrinkled face.

"You creep," shouted the young man who had ushered him into the house. Andrew was pushed off the sofa and landed on his knees on the faded carpet. The wine in his hand spilled out onto the shoes and stockings of Mrs. Jones and, as if in a dream, Andrew watched as the liquid trickled from the nylon down into her lumpy shoes. She sat as if not feeling the sensation. Perhaps she didn't.

The people around him picked him up and jostled him, not quite ready or drunk enough to strike him in front of Mrs. Jones. He was forcibly ejected from the front room and into the hallway. Many hands grabbed at him and many words were spat into his ears.   Obscenities were thrown wildly at him, his mind growing numb to the words that were used.   In a matter of seconds his jacket was torn away from him and his cartoon tie was decimated. Once Mrs. Jones was out of sight a few punches were thrown and Graham could feel blood on his face. He was becoming scared that he would be badly hurt.

Eventually he was thrown out of the front door with a large group of the Jones clan following behind him. He knew that this was where the beating would occur. He stumbled on the front step, but recovered himself enough to be able to start running away from the house. The crowd did not pursue him, perhaps in deference to their deceased relative. A few stones and rocks were thrown in his direction, one bouncing off his head and almost causing him to lose balance. Shouted insults echoed in his ears.

He didn't stop running until he reached his office building. He realised that he looked a mess. His face was bleeding and his clothes were ripped. He was sweating profusely and his stomach stuck out of his tangled shirt. He was panting and wheezing after running for so long. His face felt scarlet. He felt deeply ashamed. The Jones family had reacted naturally to him. He would have done the same. He had spoilt an important family moment and destroyed an old woman's precious memories of her husband.

He walked round the side of his office building until he stood directly below his office window. He looked round until he found the indentation in the grass where Bernard Jones had lain for two months. He lay down in the grass and started to cry.

I

The Strawberry Festival. For me, this is a phrase that stirs up feelings of happiness, nostalgia, horror, fear and suspicion. A strange combination of emotions, I'm sure you agree, so let me tell you my tale. It is the first time I've told it in public. I make no claims to it, I don't expect you to believe me. But it is true. All of it. Did I witness it all? No, but I can say that I witnessed some of the events myself and the ones that I didn't personally experience were recounted to me by reliable people. These people were, and still are, upstanding members of the community in which the events took place.

I want to set the scene before I tell my tale. I won't specifically name the town in which this happened. Too much publicity has already been given to the poor inhabitants and it isn't germane to the tale. When I have finished my tale, you'll know the place I am talking about. Suffice to say that it was the town where I was born and brought up. I left it for good when I was twenty-one years old, some twenty-five years ago. A few things have changed in the last quarter century; a new housing development or two on the outskirts, a new supermarket and a few empty shops in the town centre. But the people haven't changed. The people never change.

It is a small country town, with a population of around eight thousand. Founded in some ridiculously early century, it has a long and undistinguished history. Nothing much has happened over the centuries, a few notable people were born there and a few mildly interesting events have taken place in or near the town. It has a small town centre, with local shops and a main car park. It used to be the town green, until it was tarmacked over. The town has three schools and the main source of income for those who don't commute to the nearby large towns is agriculture. Some say that small towns hold their secrets close. I don't agree. Secrets in small towns are currency, passed around from person to person. There are very few real secrets, those that are truly hidden. This is one of them.

The Strawberry Festival was the town's celebration of the local strawberry harvest. This celebration has been around since the 1920's. It always took place on the same day in early July, which coincidentally was the same week as my birthday. It featured the Strawberry Parade, the Strawberry Queen and the Strawberry Dance. It was actually great fun, especially for the kids. The streets were decked out in red and strawberry motifs. People wore strawberry outfits and pretty much everyone in the town took the day off. Roads were closed and the celebrations lasted all day.

This tale begins in 1979. I had just turned twelve. This was the year when I started playing in one of the bands that marched in the Strawberry Parade. It was a brass band and I played second horn. It was a great feeling to be part of the event, rather than just being a member of the audience. But I digress; this isn't a biography, this is a tale about dark events.

It was on the evening of the Strawberry Festival, 1979, when the first girl disappeared. She was one of the court of the

Strawberry Queen. She was called Alison Jones and she was just seventeen years old. I have a vague recollection of her face, having seen her sitting on the float of the Strawberry Queen. My band marched directly behind this float during the parade.

At the time I was only vaguely aware of the occurrence from whispered conversations between my parents and their friends. Now I know the whole tale. I know her parents contacted the police when she hadn't returned home by midnight. The police initially took the disappearance only semi-seriously. The year 1979 may seem like a long time ago, but they weren't innocent times. Teenagers were teenagers and they still did stupid things. The police considered that the girl may have snuck off with a boyfriend or gone to a drunken house party without telling anyone. The police did some cursory investigation, but didn't probe too deeply.

Until she turned up dead the next morning.

She had been strangled and her heart neatly removed. Her corpse had been dumped on the local golf course, near to the fifth hole. The lack of blood at that location suggested that she hadn't been killed there. Naturally the townsfolk went crazy. The town had witnessed the occasional killing, but usually it was a drunken fight that got out of hand or something domestic. This was the first time that anyone had experienced an act clearly carried out by a deranged killer.

My recollection of the day that she was found is vague. I remember being ordered to stay indoors, despite the summer heat, and being allowed to watch television. I remember my father coming home early from work and my mother being tearful and upset.

The police investigation focused on Alison's family, her boyfriends and her social group at school. Teachers and school friends were quizzed, but to no avail. Local 'weirdoes' were interviewed but no-one was arrested. In those pre-DNA days, there were few clues or leads to follow-up on. I know now that the police considered it most likely that a random stranger had taken advantage of the crowd attending the Strawberry Festival to kidnap and murder. Police cars roamed the streets patrolling for any suspicious activity, whilst other officers went door-to-door asking people if they had seen or knew anything. I remember the police officer who came to see my parents. He looked dejected and bored. He was probably right to feel that way. If anyone knew anything, they would have reported it by then. Who, apart from the killer, had anything to gain by withholding information?

We were mildly thrilled to see the murder being reported on national television and in the national newspapers. A few reporters and television crews came to our town to interview the local police and town council, as well as members of the public. In a few of these shots you could see various friends of mine from school, capering around in the background. How quickly dark events are forgotten when you are twelve.

II

As summer moved towards autumn and we all went back to school, things started to calm down. Nobody had been arrested and nothing else had happened. It was a tragedy but the consensus in the town was that it had been a random stranger and that lightning didn't ever strike twice. There was some discussion about cancelling the 1980 Strawberry Festival but that was quickly dismissed. There was no reason to and it went ahead as always, during the first week of July in 1980.

Unfortunately, the lightning did strike again.

This time it was a girl called Moira Williams. She was sixteen years old. I vaguely knew her from school, but had no social interaction with her. The circumstances were the same. Exactly the same. Same mutilation, same location for dumping the body. The town went insane.

Being a bit older I remember it better. The town was flooded with police. This time they couldn't conclude that it was a random act of viciousness. Now it was a serial killer and probably some-one local. I know now from my sources that the police had withheld certain details of the first murder from the press and public. Those things were present in the second murder. It was the same guy.

The investigation ranged far and wide. Likely suspects from the whole region, as well as the town itself, were interviewed. Door-to-door interviews took place on several occasions. Anyone in the town who had the slightest possible connection with Moira were interrogated. School friends were interviewed. Her boyfriend was briefly arrested and then released almost as quickly. He and his family had to leave town after that. But nothing turned up.

I have been told by those who know about these things that random murder is the hardest to solve. Normally murder is carried out by those close to the victim; a husband, a wife, a brother, a son. And there is usually an obvious motive; money and love being the primary ones. But with random killings, it is harder to identify a motive and a likely suspect. These crimes weren't sexual in nature, the girls had not been interfered with. They were strangled and then the heart removed. The place where they were killed was not where they were found, making investigation harder. Clues were limited. No footprints, no tyre marks, no scraps of cloth or rope that could be traced. Even the blade that was likely used to remove the heart was identified as being a commonly available kitchen knife. Not exactly a surgeon's blade, but good enough to do the job.

A curfew was put in place for the duration of July, but nothing else happened. Speculation was wild, both in the town and in the wider community, including the press. The more sensational newspapers suggested that Jack the Ripper had returned, a notion that more than a few in the town took seriously.

I was thirteen when Moira was killed. I remember a sense of shock at her death, but then a growing frustration at not being allowed outside to play for the rest of the summer. My parents took me out to the seaside on occasion, but I just didn't have the freedom that I wanted to enjoy the summer properly. It is funny how quickly a tragedy turns into a selfish response, especially in a wee teenage boy.

III

The Strawberry Festival was cancelled in 1981, because it was clearly associated with the murders, but that didn't stop a third girl going missing. This time I knew her well. She also played the horn in the school band and I sat near to her every week during the school term. Her name was Deborah Carlyle. At the time she died she was only sixteen, just like Moira.

On the night she disappeared she was walking home alone from the cinema. She was found two days later. This time she wasn't left on the golf course, but instead was found in a field some three miles outside the town limits. Despite that minor difference, the police knew that it was the same murderer. He had just scored three against the town.

This time I was personally interviewed by the police. It was an unnerving event. The police interviewing me gave the impression that they knew I had committed all three murders. I guess in retrospect the police made everyone feel that way. But before you ask, this tale isn't a confession on my part. The truth of this tale is far stranger.

In 1982 and 1983 the festival was again cancelled on the advice of the police. The festival was clearly the trigger and it was best not to risk further deaths. A curfew was imposed on the day when the Strawberry Festival would have taken place. Nothing happened. From 1984 until 1986, there was still no Strawberry Festival, but no curfew was imposed. Nothing happened. In 1987, a cautious town council and local constabulary allowed the Strawberry Festival to take place. It was a very subdued affair, with no Strawberry Dance in the evening. Nothing happened. In 1988 the full Strawberry Festival took place again, including the Strawberry Dance. Nothing happened.

Whoever had killed Alison, Moira and Deborah had stopped. Nobody ever found out why.

IV

I left the town in 1989, aged twenty-one years old. I had just finished university and was off to find my place in the world. All through my undergraduate degree when I was asked where I came from my response would always illicit the same statement. Oh, you're from that town, the one where the murders took place. Then the questions would begin. Eventually I stopped telling people the truth.

I kept up to date with news from home because my parents and brother still lived there. The families of the murdered girls either moved away or, if still living in the town, were considered as perpetual objects of endless sympathy. The dead girls became part of the town's collective memory. The murders faded into the background. My generation remembered them. For the generations that came after us, the ones who were either too young or not even born at the time, the murders were part of the town folklore. It had been a black time for the town, but time does heal all things. The rawness of those three summers eased. The memories of curfews, police interviews and mutual suspicion faded. The generation who had been in their teens at the time grew old, got fat and got on with their lives. Some, like me, moved away whilst others stayed put. No doubt the murders were brought up in conversations, but only as dark reminiscences. The Strawberry Festival continued.

Then in 2009, on the evening of the Strawberry Dance, another girl went missing. She was seventeen years old and a member of the court of the Strawberry Queen, the same as the first victim way back in 1979. Her name was Alison Jones, the same as the first victim.

V

At this point I must say that I was not present for any of these later events. A friend of mine from school, who probably should remain nameless, had grown up to become an officer in the local police. I'll call him John. He was there at the climax of the tale. It was from him that I got the rest of the story.

When Alison went missing, she was lucky enough to have rather strict parents who had warned her that if she was home just one minute later than 10 p.m. then they would phone the police. An extreme reaction, no doubt, but not an uncommon one in my home town. You have to remember the parents of this generation were the grown-up versions of the children who had lived through the murders. And those murders cast a long shadow. The parents knew that on this one night in July, all the kids, but especially the daughters, had to be watched carefully. So, at 10.05 p.m., when Alison had failed to appear, her father phoned the police. And, by god, the police responded in the same way her parents had.

The police and townspeople saturated the area, looking for her. John told me that there were about fifty people waiting on the fifth hole of the golf club, just in case.

I am sure by now that you know the murders and the town that I am speaking of. And you know what happened that night in 2009. But, I suspect that you only know the official story. I know the real story and I will swear that it is the truth. It was told to me by my childhood friend, John.

You know that Alison Jones was not killed. At 11 p.m., about an hour after she went missing, the door of the town police station opened and she staggered in, distraught and dishevelled.

Of course, you all know this. In between sobs, she stammered out her story. She had been taken by a man named Alan Grayson. Who was he? Well, as you know, he was the janitor of the local secondary school. He had been around twenty years old at the time of the first murder in 1979, having taken on the janitorial role in the school he had recently just left. A lifelong bachelor, he had remained both in that job and in the town all his life. In 2009, he was just past his fiftieth birthday.

Alison told the police that she had been walking home after the Strawberry Dance had finished, keen to make it home before 10 p.m. Just as she turned a corner, she had been dragged off the street into a scruffy van, then driven to Grayson's scruffy flat, just near to the school. That was when her story got a little weird. He was a big man and had no difficulty lifting her out of the van and carrying her into his flat, where she was dumped into the bath. Now, Alison was no dummy, she knew damn well what was about to happen. She did her best to fight him off, but a swift punch to her head left her dazed and weak. But she was still conscious. Grayson stood over her, with a knife in his hand; she said his eyes were glazed and he was sweating profusely. As she waited helplessly for the end, suddenly Grayson jumped and whirled round. Alison vainly hoped that the police had discovered them and had come to rescue her. In her statement made to the police, she said that Grayson had begun a conversation with an unseen person in the flat, his arms flailing around as if to ward off some type of attack. Dropping the knife, Grayson fell to his knees, screaming in pain. That was when Alison had taken her opportunity and escaped.

Immediately after she told her tale, the police raided Grayson's home, keen to arrest him for kidnap but also to find out if he was the one responsible for the earlier murders. They suspected he was, the parallels were too similar. Now, this is point where the truth and the official versions diverge. The official report states that the police, after kicking the door in, found Grayson dead by his own hand. After searching the flat, the three missing hearts taken from the girls were found in his freezer, each in a small plastic container marked with the names Alison, Moira and Deborah. The knife that had been used to remove the hearts, a vintage kitchen knife, was found next to his body. Case closed.

But I know the real truth about what the police found and it bears only a passing resemblance to the official story. The truth was told to me one stormy night in 2013 by my friend John. We had been drinking. He was drunk enough to want to talk, but sober enough to tell the tale.

He told me that a team of five police officers had indeed arrived at Grayson's house at around 11.30 p.m. After kicking down the front door, they did find him dead on the floor of his lounge, with a knife next to him. That part of the official report was true, but it wasn't the full story. John told me the real tale, not disclosed in the report. The autopsy had proven that Grayson had not died at his own hands. He had been strangled. By small, probably female, hands. The autopsy had also shown that his heart had been removed, but there was something strange about that. Very strange. The coroner had no idea how a human heart could be removed and the body show absolutely no sign of trauma. It wasn't even as if he had been cut open and then stitched up again. His body had no cuts, no stitching; no marks of any kind. His heart was simply missing.

But it did turn up. During the search of Grayson's flat, a human heart had been found in the kitchen freezer, placed in a small plastic container labelled in a girlish script with the name Alan. It was confirmed that it belonged to Grayson. John told me that when that heart had been found, right next to it in the freezer, were three identical containers, labelled in masculine handwriting with the names Alison, Moira and Deborah. Contrary to the official report, however, all three of these containers were empty and no trace of the contents were ever found. John looked me straight in the eye and finished his tale.

"Imagine what we were feeling. Every day some further bizarre discovery was made. His heart in the freezer, but no injuries on his body. The hearts of his victims missing, but the boxes that contained them still present. We all discussed what we knew, but there was no explanation, well, no natural explanation. There was a supernatural explanation, but none of us could force ourselves to speak those thoughts out loud, even though I knew that we all were thinking the same thing."

John took another shot and looked me straight in the eye.

"I know that those girls got their hearts back on the night he died. The girls were buried without them and that must have been what they came back for. And for revenge too, of course. I think they were also driven to return because he had started again. There was no clear idea about why there had been a thirty year gap between the first and last murders, but it was probably something to do with the fact that his latest chosen victim was the same age, had the same name and was a member of the court of the Strawberry Queen. The criminal psychologists considered that those factors may have been the reason, the spark that ignited his need to kill again."

He took another shot then continued.

"I tell you, whatever they did to him before he died, it doesn't bear thinking about. The expression on his face when we found him was of sheer terror. We never reported this, of course. It would have cost us our careers. We ignored the autopsy evidence that didn't match our version of events, leaving out the part about the missing heart. Grayson was dead, the murders were solved and those poor girls could finally rest in peace. And I'm glad. Glad that he died, glad that the girls took their revenge and glad that they are all free now. But sometimes I have nightmares. Nightmares that the three will return to punish the town. The town that failed to prevent their deaths."

He sighed and took another sip of whisky.

"They might come back. That's why I still have nightmares."

The two men stood on the side of the road, next to their rental car.

"Are you sure you want to do this?" asked Brian.

"Sure, why not?" replied Peter.

"Well, because of the disappearances. For once it isn't just hearsay or old wives tales. They really happened."

"Well, that makes it definitely worth exploring. And that's what we're here for, after all."

"True," answered Brian.

Brian and Peter were old friends and colleagues. They were both academics, working in the history department of one of the major universities in Toronto. Both were nearing retirement and because of this, they both enjoyed doing absolutely nothing over the summers. Their younger colleagues, especially those who weren't tenured, used the summer break for research or conferences. Often these colleagues were busier during the summer than they were during the teaching semesters. Brian and Peter no longer felt the need to keep pushing. They were both tenured, both professors and both effectively untouchable. Now they spent their summers indulging in their mutual hobby, investigating paranormal and supernatural occurrences in southern and central Ontario. They told their wives that they were planning to write a book, but they both knew that they really just enjoyed travelling the highways and byways of Ontario, eating good food and drinking cold beer. They were keen to find evidence of the paranormal, it's just that they really weren't planning to put anything down in writing. Unless they found something, of course. Their next target, the Devil's Glen, was a likely candidate.

The Devil's Glen can be found just off Highway 124, south of Georgian Bay and the Blue Mountains in southern Ontario. It is a heavily wooded, steep ravine on the edge of hill. There is a pathway and this runs from the tarmacked road at the top to a small, dirt road at the bottom. The glen is not high on the must-see lists of tourists, mainly because there isn't much to see. And also because of its reputation. Over a period of one hundred and twenty years, seventy-two people have disappeared whilst walking in the glen.

Brian and Peter had done their homework. They knew that there were several conditions that had to be fulfilled for a disappearance to take place. Firstly, the person had to be on their own. No-one had ever disappeared if they had company. Secondly, it had to be between May and August. No-one had ever disappeared in any other month. Brian's theory was that this was when the glen was at its greenest. The leaves made it hard to see into the glen from the road above. When the leaves dropped in fall, someone looking from the road above could easily see the path that wound down the ravine to the road at the bottom. And that meant that they could keep an eye on a person walking on the path. It's hard to disappear when some-one is watching you. Thirdly, it helped if it was raining, but this wasn't a definite. Of the seventy-two missing people, fifty-three had disappeared on rainy days. For the others, it had been sunny.

And now Brian and Peter were here to investigate. It was July, it was overcast. Now they just needed to decide who would walk the path alone in the Devil's Glen. Brian smiled.

"How about a good old fashioned coin toss?"

Peter nodded. Brian removed a quarter from his pocket and tossed it in the air. Catching it deftly, he placed it on the back of his hand.

"Heads or tails?"

"Tails."

Brian exposed the coin.

"Heads it is. You get to go."

Peter was required to hand over his mobile phone before he embarked on his journey. He could only take a small notebook to record his impressions. This was something that the two friends had agreed on years before. Their investigations had to be untainted by electronic devices. It was possible that the phenomenon they investigated were electrical in origin, so they didn't want any external electronic devices affecting or ruining their observations. Peter had a theory that ghost sightings had decreased in the twenty-first century because mobile phone signals disrupted the delicate electromagnetic sources of the apparitions. Peter smiled at his friend.

"See you on the other side! I'll walk all the down to the dirt road at the bottom, then head back up here. Shouldn't take more than an hour. I may stop to make some observations, so I might be slightly longer. If I meet anybody I'll note that down."

"Okay. I'll wait here. If it rains, I'll sit in the car."

Peter walked to the edge of the path that lead down into the Devil's Glen. He felt no premonition of doom. As he headed under the canopy of green leaves he smiled back at his friend, standing at the roadside. As he stepped onto the path, Peter was struck immediately by the change in light. At the roadside the sky had been overcast, but some sunlight had managed to escape past the clouds and the day had been bright. As soon he started on the path he entered into a dim, hard-to-see world. On either side the dense foliage of the undergrowth made it hard to see even ten feet. Above him the trees grew so closely together that there was barely a glimpse of the sky. The path was clearly an old stream bed and water still trickled down, making the going wet and slippery. Peter found himself looking down to ensure that he did not slip and fall on the precipitous path. He hadn't realised just how steep it was going to be.

Brian stood at the top of the glen. He was unable to see very far down the path as it twisted and wound its way between the trees. Peter was soon lost to sight. Even standing on the edge of the path, Brian could feel the atmosphere of the place. It might have been due to the lack of sunlight or the drop in temperature or the humidity. It could even have been the slightly menacing appearance of the uncared for trees, covered in moss, or the ground covered in bushes, deadfalls and broken branches. But there was definitely something. He strained to see further down the path, whilst trying not to actually set foot on it. Without realising, his left foot slid a few inches off the roadside and onto the path. Technically, and without realising, he had just entered the Devil's Glen.

Peter reached the bottom of the glen without too much difficulty. Truth be told, he had slid most of the way, mainly on his rear-end. He now stood on a dirt road. He could see no houses. He pulled out his notebook and scratched a few thoughts. The Devil's Glen was steep, dark and damp. He had no inkling of supernatural forces on the way down. No tingles, nor neck hairs rising. Maybe it would be different on the way back up, although he suspected that his thoughts would be mainly focused on not having a heart attack as he struggled up the steep incline. He hoped Brian was ready for a beer once he made it back to the car.

It took Peter forty-five minutes to reach the top. He was slightly disappointed that he hadn't disappeared or even had the tiniest supernatural encounter. Sadly, he was forced to conclude that the Devil's Glen was not somewhere that he would consider to be haunted. Perhaps the disappeared people had simply strayed off the path, or had even fallen and ended up in the thick undergrowth? That seemed the likeliest explanation.

As he reached the top of the glen, the slope became less steep and he realised that it was getting brighter. After a couple more minutes he could see the bright circle that was the end of the path. He had hoped to see Brian standing waiting for him, but he wasn't there. That was odd; the Devil's Glen did have a real history of disappearances and he thought Brian just might have been worried enough to hang around the entrance, rather than just wandering off to the look at the local flora or sit in the car.

Peter reached the roadside where the car was parked. It was empty. Blinking in the sunlight, he looked up and down the road. He saw no sign of his friend. He walked down the road for a short distance, then back to the car. He walked in the opposite direction, looking at the edges of the road to see if Brian was in the ditch for some reason.

After a frustrating few minutes he walked back to the start of the path into the

Devils' Glen. Was it possible that Brian had headed down the ravine himself? He looked down. There were some footprints in the dry dust at the edge of the path. There were his footprints, leading down and then back up. The only other footprint was the front part of a boot, just at the edge of the pathway, a footprint that bore the distinctive track marks of the hiking boots that Brian invariably wore. Nothing else. It was then that the truth hit Peter. The Devil's Glen had just taken its seventy third victim.

It was often said that William was a young man with an old man's personality. That wasn't strictly true. He liked old things, collected them, but he also loved technology and kept up to date with the latest smart phones and other modern devices. He considered himself to be some-one who straddled the worlds of both old and new, enjoying and appreciating both equally.

Take his love of photography. He collected all the latest digital cameras, but also loved to browse antique shops for vintage cameras and vintage photograph albums. Some of the albums he collected already contained photographs and some didn't. He used the ones that didn't have photographs to display the photographs that he himself had taken. A fan of electronic media, he still valued the physical reality of a photograph.

His wife, Fiona, was well used to William enthusiastically showing her the latest purchase from one of his usual antique shops. On this occasion it was a rather musty vellum photograph album. Its leather cover was burgundy in colour and highlighted with gilt flourishes. Inside the vellum was creamy and rich. Even to her non-expert eye it was clearly Victorian.

"Looks very nice," she said.

"It's paper vellum, rather than hide, but it's still very good quality. It's a shame that all the photographs have been removed, it would have been interesting to see the family who owned such an expensive, handmade photograph album. But I thought that it would be perfect for our next volume of family photographs."

"Yes, it probably will, but it does smell a little musty."

"Oh don't worry about that. I'll air it out before I mount any photographs."

She smiled. A nice harmless hobby for a nice harmless husband. William headed to his little cubbyhole where he stored his collectibles, both modern and old. It was, in reality, the third bedroom. The shelves were cluttered with a range of different objects and books. In the middle of this seeming chaos, there was a neat desk. His desk. He sat.

He placed the vellum photograph album on the desk and simply stared at it. It was nice just to look at these antique objects, savouring the feeling that he was the latest in a long line of custodians of this object. He considered that he didn't own these objects, he was just being given the gift of looking after them until he could pass it onto the next curator.

Since this was going to be the vehicle for the next set of family snaps, William leaned back and selected a box from the shelf directly behind him. This box contained the latest batch of family photographs. Well, not really family, since it was only himself and Fiona. No kids yet. He browsed briefly through the box and selected a photograph of the firm's last Christmas party. He and Fiona had met in the sales office of the local plastics firm. After their marriage she had initially gone part time, then ultimately she had given up, preferring life as a housewife. He didn't mind, his salary sufficed for their modest lifestyle. He had taken Fiona to the last party, partly because he liked to share everything in his life with her and partly because she still knew a number of people at the firm. Some of his colleagues preferred not to take their partners, just in case an 'opportunity' presented itself.

The photograph he selected showed four people. He and Fiona were in the middle. Beside him was a lady called Marge, one of Fiona's old colleagues. Next to Fiona was Kevin, one of the guys in the sales office. Kevin was a bit brash for William's taste, but you couldn't expect to like everyone in the workplace. It was a perfectly ordinary photograph showing four slightly inebriated people wearing stupid party hats at a perfectly ordinary work Christmas do, but since Fiona looked so happy and carefree he decided to make it the first photograph in the album.

He placed the photograph carefully into the vellum album, positioning it carefully in the middle of the first page. He glanced sideways to grab some tape to stick the photograph down. As he glanced back his heart almost stopped.

The photograph had changed.

Not completely. The four people were still there, wearing stupid hats. He looked the same as before, as did Marge. But the expressions on the faces of Fiona and Kevin were different. Instead of smiling directly at the camera, Fiona was now looking directly at William with an expression of pure hatred. Her upper lip was curled up in disgust and her eyes were half closed with distaste. The expression on Kevin's face was pure lust as he gazed at Fiona. Pure unadulterated lust. William started uncontrollably. He grabbed the photo from the album and dropped it onto the desk in front of him. He gasped. It was back to normal.

Now, William was a rational individual, not prone to excessive flights of imagination. As a child he had not dreamt of Narnia or other magical worlds, instead preferring the solid reality of building blocks and train sets. After his initial shock he did some thinking. Could he have imagined the change? Well, obviously yes. Could the change be real? Well, obviously no. Photographs didn't change to show rather vile expressions, and then change back to normal again. He must be tired or stressed of something, even though he felt normal. Perhaps he was spending too much time with musty old antiques.

He picked out another photo from the box and placed it into the vellum album. This photo was one of himself and Fiona at the seaside last summer. It was a pleasant photograph. They were on the pier and the background to the photograph was the town, rather than the sea. It had been taken by a passer-by. He rather gingerly stared at the photograph, despite his rational mind telling him he was being stupid. After a few seconds nothing had happened so he turned round to pick up the fixing tape. When he turned back his heart sank. Rather than smiling happily, the photograph now showed Fiona sneering in what could only be called disgust at him. He closed his eyes then opened them again. The photograph hadn't changed back to normal and even worse, the first photograph, which he had just placed back into the album, showed those terrible, terrible facial expressions again. He stared and stared, but this time they did not change. He picked the first photo up and held it close to his face, to try and see if it been tampered with. It was back to normal. He put it on his desk. Still normal. He placed it back into the album. The vile facial expressions were back. Could it be the album?

Over the next few hours he experimented. Digging out all the photographs from the Christmas party, he selected all the photographs that had either himself, Fiona or Kevin. He worked out something interesting. The photograph had to feature a combination of himself, Fiona or Kevin for any change to take place. If it was himself and Fiona, then she looked disgusted at being in his presence. If it was himself and Kevin, then Kevin looked with anger and hate at him. If the photograph had Fiona and Kevin then the primary emotion was lust. Between Fiona and Kevin.

When removed from the album, the photographs went back to being normal, relatively boring photographs. William, a tirelessly logical person, could only conclude one thing. That somehow the vellum album was reading the real emotions behind the photographs. Some force was reading the truth and expressing it by changing the subjects' faces to show their real emotions. Their real feelings. Their real relationships. But he didn't believe his conclusion. It wasn't possible. It couldn't be.

Over the next few weeks Fiona noticed changes in her husband's personality. William wasn't exactly an extrovert, but she noticed that he was becoming more and more withdrawn. In the evenings he gulped his meals without conversation and then disappeared to his cubby hole. He even slept there sometimes, clearing a space for himself on the tiny, single bed. They barely spoke in the morning or at weekends. William was looking drawn and tired, dark bags under his eyes. Fiona was increasingly worried.

So was William, but for different reasons. His wife was screwing Kevin behind his back. The photographs were telling the truth. He didn't know how and he didn't know why, but somehow the album changed the photographs to show the true emotions of the people in them. Night after night, day after day he sat in the third bedroom and put photographs of himself, Fiona and Kevin into the vellum album. Night after night, day after day the photographs changed to more and more obscene and disgusting images. Images of lust, hatred, jealousy and perversion. They haunted his dreams and bled into his waking world. Kevin and Fiona. Kevin and Fiona. Kevin and Fiona.

Well, he decided. Now that he knew the truth, there wouldn't be any Kevin and Fiona for much longer.

Detective Inspector Thomson looked down at the huddled corpses and shook his head.

"Murder then suicide?"

Detective Sergeant Forbes nodded.

"Killed her then himself. The note says she was having an affair with some guy at his workplace."

"Was she?"

"No, we sent Smith over to check. This guy, Kevin Masterson is happily married and barely knew the deceased. People in the office confirm this; there were no hints, whispers or rumours and that is the sort of thing that would be an open secret. It's pretty obvious that this was something this guy here made up all by himself."

"And he killed her, just because of something he imagined?"

"Looks like it."

"Where on earth do these nuts get these delusions from?"

Forbes just shook his head slowly.

Wayne stared over the garden wall at the kid and his puppy playing on the lawn of the big house. Wayne decided that he wanted the puppy. He'd been walking the streets all day, unsuccessfully looking for somewhere to rob. He was tired and hot and in a bad mood. Seeing that little kid on the immaculate lawn of that expensive house with the cute puppy made him mad. If he couldn't rob somewhere, he might as well take the puppy. Could have some fun with it, then sell it or dump it. He vaulted over the wall and stood for a brief second in the bushes, scouting out the scene. The kid was by himself, playing with the puppy. No adults. He walked over to the kid, a boy of about five years old.

"Hey kid. Nice puppy."

The little boy looked up and smiled.

"He's mine. He's called Spot."

If the boy had been just a little bit older he would have known that Wayne, dressed in a shell-suit and cheap trainers, was probably up to no good. The outfit marked Wayne out as some-one who would never be able to afford a big house in a nice neighbourhood like this one. Wayne stared down at the boy, feeling his mood get darker. But then a voice spoke, the source right next to Wayne's left ear.

"Don't Wayne. Don't do what you're planning to do."

He whirled round, his sharpened and experienced fight or flight instinct causing the instant reaction. There was no-one there. He flexed his arms, the gold rings on his fingers winking in the sun. The tattoos on his knuckles, once a novelty but now so familiar that he no longer noticed them, moved as he cracked his knuckles. The boy just sat and stared at him. Sweat broke out on Wayne's forehead. He was not the most imaginative person and that voice had freaked him out. He felt an overwhelming urge to punch the boy. Hard. The voice spoke again.

"You really don't want to that, Wayne. Not a nice idea."

"What the hell?"

He whirled around again, but there was still nothing there. The boy, still sitting on the grass, giggled.

"It ain't funny, you little tosser," shouted Wayne, finally grateful for an excuse to vent his anger. He pulled back his fist to punch the kid.

"*I wouldn't…*," said the voice in a sing-song manner.

Wayne's hand fell to his side. Screw this, he thought to himself. Just grab the puppy and go. Bending, he pushed the little kid out of the way; the kid started to snuffle. Wayne reached out to pick up the puppy.

"*You don't want to do that, Wayne. I really wouldn't.*"

"Who's talking? Who keeps talking to me?"

The little boy, still lying prone, spoke up.

"It's nanny. She looks after us when we are playing. She stops any bad people. Bad people like you."

"Nanny?"

"Nanny," said the boy with just a trace of smugness in his voice.

"Just give me the bloody dog, mate."

Wayne grabbed the puppy roughly, so that it squealed in pain and distress. There was a sudden growl from behind him. Wayne's eyes locked with the boy's.

"Nanny is here."

The child cocked his head to one side, a curiously adult gesture.

"And do you want to know a secret."

"What?" asked Wayne, frozen in place by the staring, smiling child and by the growl. He wasn't sure he wanted to see what had made the noise. The puppy, squirmed in his hand and he tightened his grip, making it squeal again.

"She's my nanny, but she is also Spot's mummy. And she doesn't like it when Spot squeals. When people are horrid to us."

Wayne turned round. The dog, the one that he had failed to see when he first entered the garden, stood two feet away from him, its teeth bared. It was a bigger, a much bigger, version of the puppy that he was still holding and its teeth were *huge*. The dog, this bitch, looked at the puppy and nodded imperceptibly. Wayne dropped the puppy; it bumped onto the ground and, unhurt, ran back to the little boy. Then the nanny took a step forward.

Wayne had the briefest moment to regret his actions, regret his life, and realise that sometimes, just sometimes, karma really does bite you in the ass.

I often find that some notes about the author and the book that I have just finished reading are both useful and illuminating, so I decided to write some notes for you, dear reader. However the biggest question is what to write? Well, let's start with the basics. I have been writing for a long time, nearly twenty years in fact, but this is my first book. The stories in this collection are both old and new. A few were written nearly twenty years ago, whilst others were written just this year. I've written many, many stories over the last twenty years, most of which will never see the light of day. I've selected what I think are some of my best stories for this collection, a bold claim no doubt, especially if you don't like *any* of them.

The last twenty years, as well as being the time frame in which these stories were written, was also a period that saw many changes in my life. A couple of job changes and a couple of location changes, including one rather large move from the U.K. to Canada.

It is for this reason that the stories in the collection are sometimes set in the U.K. and sometimes set in Canada. An author must write what they know and what they experience. They were all selected for inclusion in this collection because I felt that they fitted the overall theme that I wanted, which was a mixture of stories with supernatural and macabre themes.

The themes of these tales are quite dark. Cannibalism, vampires, revenge from beyond the grave, death and the devil feature in these stories. Some are ghost stories, some are merely macabre and some feature other aspects of the supernatural. But I don't think the stories aren't entirely dark. There are some uplifting moments, I hope. I think it is quite possible for supernatural tales to have happy endings.

A question I'm sometimes asked is whether or not I believe in ghosts and the supernatural. The answer is a sad no. But I've always enjoyed stories of the ghosts, ghoulies and the supernatural. One of my favourite hobbies is collecting, reading and enjoying rare ghost stories. Authors such as

M.R. James, August Derleth, Ramsay Campbell and Basil Copper have all inspired me.

Although I don't believe, a small part of me wishes that it was true. That in certain houses the phantoms of previous owners still wander after midnight, that deserted railway stations still have ghostly arrivals after the station is closed, that the dead still remember the living. It's a nice idea; a comforting idea. I also think that the thrill of the supernatural is such an innate part of the human condition that stories of ghosts and the supernatural will never die. For one, I am glad about this.

Some of the places in the stories are real. The glen in 'The Devil's Glen' is real. It lies near Georgian Bay in Ontario, fairly close to where I now live. The unnamed town in 'The Strawberry Festival' is based on my home town and the summer festival that takes place every year, although, of course, the story itself is entirely fictional. The Victorian clockwork toy mentioned in 'Mr Todd' is also entirely real and yes, it did terrify me as a child.

So, finally some thanks and acknowledgements. Firstly, thanks to WolfStar Publishing for agreeing to publish this collection. Their support is much appreciated. Thanks to my family, especially Sally, for allowing me the many hours that it took to write and edit these tales. Thanks to my parents who set me forth on the path of loving books and reading, and who let me read all those ghost stories when I was younger. And a final thanks to you, dear reader, for taking the time to read these stories. You never know, one day we may meet again.

R.J. Meldrum

June 2015